W9-BXR-786

TWEEN FICTION K

WHILE YOU WERE OUT

WHILE YOU WERE OUT

J. Irvin Kuns

DUTTON CHILDREN'S BOOKS ❏ NEW YORK

CIP Data is available.

Published in the United States by Dutton Children's Books,
a division of Penguin Young Readers Group
345 Hudson Street, New York, New York 10014
www.penguin.com

Designed by Irene Vandervoort
Printed in USA
First Edition

ISBN 0-525-47295-9

1 3 5 7 9 10 8 6 4 2

❑ ACKNOWLEDGMENTS

"Come to the edge," He said.
They said, "We are afraid."
"Come to the edge," He said.
They came.
He pushed them . . . and they flew.
— GUILLAUME APOLLINAIRE

Chris Lynch was the first to beckon. Sharon Darrow, Brock Cole, and Jane Resh Thomas persisted. Collectively they gave me the old heave-ho. I am eternally grateful to my courageous and wise Vermont College mentors.

I would also like to thank Anita Riggio, Bruce Black, Ann Angel, and Leigh Fenly for their unrelenting friendship, moral support, and eagle-eyed critiques, along with the rest of the students and faculty of Vermont College's MFA in Writing for Children and Young Adults program, past and present, each a piece of the process.

Thanks to my mom, Alice Irvin, for keeping her feet on the ground and my children under her wing; to my husband, Brett, for his financial backing despite the occasional turbulence; to Andrew for his remarkable big-brother example; and to my loyal scribes, Grant, Emily, and Gavin.

Finally, thanks to Shelly Coppola for her excellent navigational skills, and to Dr. Joel Rudinger, who pointed to the cliff.

In loving memory of Dad and Ron

I had been my whole life a bell, and never knew it until at that moment I was lifted and struck.

—ANNIE DILLARD,
Pilgrim at Tinker Creek

❑ CONTENTS

WHILE YOU WERE OUT

GREEN FROGS AND LEAD TWINKIES

THE KITCHEN FLOOR FELT COLD beneath my bare feet as I stood in the middle of it, hugging my elbows and watching my father pace.

Dad glanced at me. "Okay, I guess I am a little nervous about this new job," he admitted.

Normally, I didn't care what Dad did for a living, but today was different. Today Dad started a new job as the school janitor. The school janitor at *my* school.

Dad jingled his pocket change and continued pacing. "I almost feel like a kid myself about to begin my first day at a new school. I don't know anyone, don't know the routine. I *do* know where the bathrooms are, though." Dad forced out a little chuckle.

Blue strawberries dotted my pajamas. I studied them, wondering if I should remind Dad about Poetry Therapy.

Mom had signed me up for a six-week course after my friend Tim died. They taught us to give names to our feelings. The counselor said by naming them we "made them ours" and could somehow understand them better. It never seemed to work for me, but mine was a much more serious case. It might work for something as silly as first-day-on-the-job jitters.

Outside, the sun was just beginning to pull itself up over the tops of the cornstalks. I took a deep breath.

"Today my name is Yellow Hope," I lied.

Dad stopped pacing. "Excuse me?"

"It's Poetry Therapy, Dad. Remember? You're supposed to name your feelings."

"Oh yeah, that. Wait, don't tell me." He held up his hand like a crossing guard. "Let me see if I can remember how it goes." He pursed his lips. "I'm feeling a little nervous today, a little jumpy. And I'm feeling a bit like a greenhorn since I've never done this type of work before. Hmm . . . jumpy and green . . ." He snapped his fingers. "I've got it. Today my name is Green Frog." He winked.

"Not bad for starters, Dad, but keep practicing. You never know when you're really going to need it."

"Wait a minute," he said slowly, cocking his head. "I

know I'm new at this Poetry Therapy stuff, but you don't look like Yellow Hope to me. Care to try it again?"

I sighed. I couldn't get anything by him. "Today my name is Lead Twinkie," I admitted. I felt like I had swallowed one whole, and it lay in the bottom of my stomach like a sunken submarine.

Dad got this look on his face like he had gas or something. He pulled me toward him. "Come on, now," he said, squeezing blue strawberries on my shoulder. "I have a feeling fifth grade is going to be great." But by the sound of his croak and the look in his green, froggy eyes, I had a feeling he didn't believe that any more than I did.

"But right now this Green Frog needs to jump-start the car," he said, tousling my hair. "And I need a lead-footed Twinkie to help me. Come on."

I followed him out the back door. Dad knew a lot about cars. He'd buy them junked and cheap, then patch them up, get them running again, and sell them for a small profit. Most of the time I never saw Dad whole; either his head was gone, hidden under the hood of one old car, or the entire top half of his body disappeared beneath another. Instead of yellow daffodils, red tulips, and green grass, the first signs of spring at our house were yellow, red, and green cars sinking in the mud of our driveway, awaiting resurrection. I was eight before I realized that the fresh smell of spring everyone was always chirping about wasn't the blended aromas of gasoline, oil, and exhaust fumes.

Dad grabbed the jumper cables out of the old red station wagon as I took my place behind the wheel. The station wagon was my favorite of all the beat-up old cars that littered our yard. It had a hole in the floor of the backseat. Whenever we rode in it, Tim and I used to pretend we were Fred and Wilma Flintstone, and that we had to stick our feet down through the hole and run real fast to get the car going. It wasn't far from the truth. Tim and I had helped push-start many a car.

Dad eased Mom's car up until it was nose to nose with the station wagon. He lifted the hoods of each, then clamped on the cables.

"Okay, try it," he called, his voice muffled from under the hood. I turned the key, but the engine just clicked.

Dad adjusted a cable. "Try her again," he ordered.

I turned the key again. This time the car came to life.

"Gun it!" Dad yelled. I stretched my body out straight as a broom, pointed my right foot, and pressed the gas pedal. Black smoke rose up around the car as the engine coughed, sputtered, then roared. I pinched my nose and breathed through my mouth.

"Okay, okay, that's good." Dad pulled his head out of the gaping mouth of the station wagon, unclamped the cables, and dropped the hood of the car with a bang. He wiped his hands quickly on a greasy black rag.

I slid out of the car, holding the door for him. "Dad, are you going to stop fixing up old cars now that you have a real job?"

"Nah, probably not. But at least now I'll be able to pay the bills without relying on used-car sales."

Or on Mom? I thought, but bit my tongue.

Mom said Dad was a good worker, just restless, and that he had a hard time finding a job that fit him. So, like me shopping for the perfect-fitting jeans, he tried on lots of them. He'd stay for a week or two, then pick up his paycheck and quit. He joked about it sometimes. "Jack-of-all-trades, master of none," he'd say with a laugh. But I knew he wished he were master of something. Anything. But he wasn't.

The problem was, Dad would rather be painting than doing anything else. But painting pictures didn't pay the bills either, so when Lester retired as janitor at my school, Dad applied. How long would this job last?

"Well, I'd better get going before she dies again," Dad said. "Thanks for your help, Twinkie. See you at school."

I watched him roar away in a cloud of exhaust.

He'll see me at school!

The lead Twinkie rolled over in my stomach as I suddenly realized the injustice of it all. Today I started school with my dad instead of with my best friend.

❏ 2

PUFFS OF MEMORIES

I WENT BACK to my room and had a stare-down with the cow painted on my bedroom wall. It had been a dreary November Saturday when Dad got bored and decided to transform my bedroom into a pasture. He covered one entire wall, floor to ceiling, corner to corner, with cows, green grass, and a split-rail fence.

Tim and I had been sitting on my bed, watching Dad work. Dad made it look so easy. He'd just dip into the reddish brown paint, sweep his brush over the wall, and suddenly a narrow dirt road appeared, wriggling in the wake of the paintbrush. He twisted the brush, making the road thinner and thinner until it finally disappeared completely over the top of a hill. "The road to freedom is always up," Dad quoted.

"Yeah, plus you gotta watch out for cow pies," Tim had warned.

When Dad had finished the cows, Tim looked at me, scrunched his eyebrows, and asked, "Why do cows wear bells?"

Tim was always asking me questions like that. Questions about things I had never really thought about until he made me think about them. And so I thought about it, long and hard. I hated giving up. Why *do* cows wear bells? Finally I shrugged. "I give up."

"Because their horns don't work. Duh, Penelope." I punched him, and he laughed and rolled into a ball, the bed squeaking as if it were giggling, too.

Tim and I had been best friends since preschool. Then, at the end of fourth grade, he left me, "after a brave battle with bone cancer." Now, every time I looked at the mural, I wished I could just step right into that pasture, cow pies and all, and shuffle up that long skinny road, scuffing up a cloud of dust and never looking back.

"You win," I told the staring cow. "I have to get ready for school."

I knelt next to Squeaky and slid the shoebox out from underneath. I had named my bed "Squeaky" during my very first Poetry Therapy session. That same day I named my bike "Breeze," my house "Pink Palace," and my neighbor Diane "Birdlips." I was off to a productive start.

As I lifted the lid and rustled my new shoes out of the tissue, I had to admit there were some good things about the first day of school. The shoes were stiff and solid, smelling of new leather. The laces were clean and still flat, having been tied only once so far at the shoe store.

Tim used to stash stuff under his big hospital bed, too. It was so high, there was plenty of room. When Dr. Murphy finally released him from St. Anne's, Tim got to take the bed home with him. It was too big to get upstairs, so his parents set it up in their den. I visited Tim there every day and stayed until his mom told me he needed to rest. Tim looked small in that big bed. And bored. So sometimes I pretended we were at a carnival and the bed was a ride. I'd crank up the head of the bed, then crank down the foot, then make the whole thing flat. Up and down. Up and down. I pretended to be a carny, grabbing a black licorice stick from the candy jar by his bed and letting it hang out the side of my mouth like a cigarette. I'd say, "Step right up, git yer tickets here," my licorice cigarette bouncing with every word. I know I had more fun than Tim did, though. He was the one who got to ride, but a ride is no fun if you can't get off.

Tim got gifts all the time when he was sick. Matchbox cars, baseball cards, squirt guns, boomerangs, marbles, and games like Scrabble and Battleship. People gave him books with big, beautiful, shiny pictures in them. The books smelled as good as they looked. I'd open them, stick my nose deep inside, and just breathe.

After he died, Tim's parents put all of the stuff from under his bed into a big box and gave it to me. Then they moved away. I stared at my closet door. That box was still in there. I had shoved it all the way to the back and hadn't looked at it since.

I turned back to the shoes, flipped them over, and ran my palm across the clean, smooth soles. No dings. No scrapes. No tar or gum. No memories. A clean slate.

I named them Slick and Smooth.

Birdlips was already perched at the kitchen table and squawking away by the time Slick and Smooth carried me down to breakfast. Birdlips was the perfect name for Diane because she had no lips. Her mouth was just one straight line like I used to draw on my stick figures in kindergarten. That is, when her mouth was shut, which wasn't very often. And since she lived next door, just an acre of garden away, she was always swooping in and hovering over me like a seagull at the beach when it thinks you have a morsel of something it wants.

Mom placed a box of Cocoa Puffs on the table when she

saw me coming. She never bought "junk cereal" except on special occasions. I guess she figured that the first day of a new school year was something to celebrate. I sure didn't feel like celebrating anything, but I wasn't about to argue—I had my Cocoa Puffs.

I plopped down at the table and tipped the box, watching the first few puffs rattle into the bowl. I kept pouring until I had a small pitcher's mound. When milk was added, the whole heap rose like homemade bread. A few Cocoa Puffs escaped over the sides of the bowl. I stuffed a huge spoonful into my mouth.

"There's milk running down your chin," Birdlips pointed out.

"Good morning to you, too," I said, but with a mouthful of Cocoa Puffs it came out sounding more like, "Goo moo, tutu." More milk dribbled out, but I didn't care. I wanted to cram as many of the delicious chocolaty morsels into my mouth as I possibly could. With a mouthful, I could better appreciate the Cocoa Puffy aroma. I crunched once, breathed deeply through my nose, crunched again. I'd forgotten how rough fresh Cocoa Puffs were. They scraped the roof of my mouth.

Darn it. Cocoa Puffs reminded me of Tim, too. I stopped chewing.

Concentrate on the Cocoa Puffs.

I decided to let them soak and soften in my mouth for a few seconds. I rolled them around, trying to count them with my tongue, then divided them into equal parts on each side of my mouth. I wanted them to make contact with every single taste bud available.

It was no use. I gave up and let the memories come.

I remembered the Cocoa Puffs cramming contests Tim and I used to have. Whoever got the most Cocoa Puffs into his mouth without laughing and spewing them all over won.

And then there was the time Tim got a rabbit for his birthday. He had to explain to his baby brother that those really weren't Cocoa Puffs in the bottom of the cage and that he shouldn't eat them. I smiled, causing more milk to escape. Finally, I swallowed and wiped my chin on my sleeve.

Mom watched me over the brim of her coffee cup.

"Well, Penelope, I guess you and I will have to go back to writing our *While You Were Out* notes to keep in touch now, huh?" She smiled a sad smile at me.

The *While You Were Out* slips were supposed to be used for missed phone calls. I used them for missed Moms.

Mom worked second shift as a unit secretary at the hospital. Second shift meant three o'clock in the afternoon until eleven-thirty at night. Since I didn't get home from school until three forty-five, and since eleven-thirty was way past my bedtime, during the week we didn't see much of each other. We were like ships passing in the night, she said.

Mom tried to get up early enough to see me off to school, but I knew it was hard for her. By the time she got home from work, it was almost midnight. Then she needed time to "unwind," as she called it. She would warm up the leftovers from supper, then watch the late show. Sometimes she threw in a load of laundry if I told her that I absolutely must have my black jeans by tomorrow. A lot of times she didn't get to bed until two or three o'clock in the morning. Once I even found her asleep in the chair when I got up for school.

"At least this year you'll have your dad around to keep you company." Mom tried to sound cheerful. The lead Twinkie rolled again. I looked at Mom and returned the sad smile.

"Well, I'd better go get dressed," Mom said. "I have to get groceries before work today. Have a great day, girls."

Halfway up the stairs she called back, "And keep an eye out for that bus. On the first day, you never know when it'll show up."

Like the early bird after the worm, Birdlips swooped in. "What did she mean by that?"

"She meant, on the first day of school you never know when the bus'll show up. It was pretty clear to me, Birdli— Diane."

"Not that. I mean the part about having your dad keep you company."

I quickly shoveled in another huge bite of Cocoa Puffs so I wouldn't have to answer.

Birdlips persisted. "Is your dad a teacher? Is somebody leaving? I hope it's Mrs. Potter. She doesn't let us get away with anything when she's cafeteria monitor. No wait! Better yet, your dad's going to be the principal and we're getting rid of Ms. Cordle!"

I gave her a "get real" look and kept chewing.

"Okay, so that's not it, either." She thought for a minute. "I've got it. Your dad's the cook. No more Mrs. Haskins. And he'll make those really good fried potatoes for us."

I shook my head and pinned a Cocoa Puff to the bottom of the bowl with my spoon.

"The bus driver?" she asked, losing hope.

I released the Cocoa Puff. It bobbed to the surface. I swallowed, wiped my chin again, and sighed. "He's the janitor," I said quietly.

Birdlips flapped her wings and practically flew off the chair. "What? You're kidding! The janitor? At our school?

Your dad?" She acted as if I had told her Homer Simpson was taking the job.

I shot BBs at her with my eyes. Finally, her birdbrain grasped the idea that it might be wise to drop the subject. She brushed her cheek with the end of her braid, which usually meant she was thinking and which always made me nervous. Suddenly she sat up straight and tilted her head.

"Is that the bus I hear?"

"Couldn't be," I said. I had just poured a fresh bowl of Cocoa Puffs. Besides, it wasn't supposed to be here for another ten minutes.

"You'd better check," she said. "You heard your mom. 'On the first day, you never know when it'll show up.'"

I shrugged. It wouldn't hurt to let my freshly poured Cocoa Puffs tenderize for a few minutes longer. I went to the front picture window where another one of Dad's painting projects greeted me. When lightning had struck the window, it left a big jagged crack that sprouted from the bottom left corner, then darted diagonally all the way to the top right corner. Dad couldn't afford to replace it, so he painted the whole crack green, like a vine, then added leaves to make it look like ivy. At Christmas, he dabbed on some red berries, transforming the ivy to holly. I stooped to peer under the camouflaged crack. Nothing but cornfields.

"No bus," I said, sliding back into my chair. "Must have been a garbage truck or something." I scooped up another heaping spoonful of Cocoa Puffs. Yes. Better. Softer.

Then I saw it.

Diane's bowl was heaped to overflowing with Cocoa Puffs. The now almost empty box lay on its side, spilling the last few precious Cocoa Puffs onto the table.

"I just got an idea," she said. "Let's have a Cocoa Puffs cramming contest like you and Tim used to." She scooped up a spoonful, leaned over her bowl, and looked at me. "Ready?" she asked, opening her mouth wide.

"No!" I grabbed her wrist and twisted, forcing her to dump her spoonful of Cocoa Puffs back into the bowl.

"Okay, okay, bad idea," she said, rubbing her wrist.

"I'm going to go wait for the bus," I snapped. I snatched my book bag off the counter and stomped for the door.

How dare she? Cocoa Puff cramming contests were something Tim and I invented. No one had Cocoa Puff cramming contests but us.

As I passed the telephone table in the front hall, I grabbed the pink *While You Were Out* message pad lying there and shoved it into my pocket. I wish Birdlips would stay in her own nest. Somebody ought to clip her wings. I marched to the end of the driveway, set my book bag down firmly in the grass, plopped myself down on it, hugged my knees, and studied my new shoes. The toes were wet with the morning dew and crisscrossed with grass clippings. Slick and Smooth were spoiled already.

The cardboard backing of the message pad jabbed my thigh. I pulled it out.

In second grade, when I first started using *While You Were Out* notes, my sloppy writing spelled out stupid things like *Dear Mom, I miss you. Love, P.* Or *Dear Mom, Dad ate all the chocolate-chip cookies. Can we make more?* Now I had much more important things to say. I dug a pen out of my book bag and wrote.

FOR Mom   URGENT ☒

FROM Me

MESSAGE Stop feeding the birds!

All of a sudden, I felt a crawly feeling come over me as if someone, or something, was watching. Very slowly I turned and looked behind me. There he was, not ten feet away, glaring at me, head cocked as if daring me to make a move. I held my breath. Ares.

I had named this rooster after our unit on Greek gods.

Ares, we had learned, was the god of war. He was mean and brutal and aggressive, a description that fit this rooster perfectly. But Ares, the god of war, was also a coward, and so far Ares, the rooster, hadn't shown that side of himself.

The funny thing was, I had never really noticed this rooster until Tim got sick. I had just returned from visiting Tim once when I found Ares smack-dab in the middle of my front yard. He had planted himself dead center between me and the safety of my house. I remembered how he had looked at me that day, cocking his head and staring at me with one red beady eye. Both of us stood frozen, him out of stubbornness, me out of fear.

Then, a few weeks later, the topper. I was in the henhouse gathering eggs and had stooped to study this one egg in particular. It was all bumpy and lopsided, and I wondered if it might be one of those eggs with the double yolks. Suddenly I had that feeling again—that feeling of being watched. I turned my head, and into the corner of my eye stepped Ares. Slowly I placed the lumpy egg in the basket. *Just stay calm,* I told myself. *No quick moves and everything will be fine.* The next thing I knew, the crazed beast was on my back. Sharp claws pierced my skin as he gripped my T-shirt. Wings wildly flapping, he seemed to be trying to carry me off somewhere, like the flying monkeys in *The Wizard of Oz.*

Feathers flew around my head, reminding me of the pillow fights I used to have with Tim. I screamed and jumped up so quickly Ares went flying backward. I could hear him thump as he hit the wall of the henhouse. I was out of there in a heartbeat, and my heart was beating plenty fast by then. Ever since that day, I often noticed him lurking behind a tree or around the corner of the house—just watching and waiting.

The front door banged shut and Diane emerged. Ares strutted away. Did he leave because now there were two of us? Or did he leave because one of the two of us was Diane? Maybe Ares *was* a coward, after all. But whatever he was, he wasn't stupid.

❏ 3
A LONG RIDE

THE BUS SCREECHED to a stop in front of me. I stood, crammed the pink pad back into my pocket, stepped up to the bus, and reached for the silver bar to the left of the door. As I hoisted myself up the three giant steps, Mr. Rockwell nodded at me, checked his clipboard, and said, "Seat number three, kiddo."

Good. Assigned seats. This way it was up to Mr. Rockwell to decide who would sit with me. And his doing if I ended up sitting alone. Kids couldn't stare and cup their hands and whisper about feeling sorry for me because I had no friends left. It was just the seating chart.

I plopped onto the third seat and inched myself toward the window with my hands. On the shiny silver surface of the back of the seat in front of me, someone had scratched SARAH LOVES MIKE. I remembered Tim staring and frowning at scratches on the back of another seat when we were riding home one day last winter. He had looked confused. Finally, he turned to me and asked, "Penelope, is *s-u-x* a word?" I smiled, remembering. The smile quickly disappeared when I heard Mr. Rockwell's voice again.

"Seat number three, Diane," he said, pulling the silver handle, closing the doors and trapping us inside.

No!

Suddenly I was back under that metal washtub where Diane and her brothers had pinned me once when I was little. It was so tight, my elbows touched both sides of the tub. This bus was roomier than that tub had been, but I felt just as trapped.

Everything was wrong. It was Tim who was supposed to share a bus seat with me, not Diane. It was Tim who was supposed to be sitting in my kitchen cramming Cocoa Puffs with me, definitely not Diane. Wait a minute . . . She didn't think she was going to replace Tim, did she? Did she think she could just swoop in now and become my new instant friend? No one could replace Tim. Friends like Tim came along once in a lifetime. What nobody seemed to understand was that I wasn't even interested in making new friends, anyway. I had been given my shot at a best friend and I lost him. I had used up my best-friend quota.

Birdlips landed beside me, bouncing me right off the seat.

"I get to sit with you, Penelope!" she chirped.

"Super," I said without a trace of enthusiasm.

"I've got a joke for you. Why do they make school bus seats green?"

"Why?" I turned away to stare out the window.

"So when kids wipe their boogers on the seats, you can't see them." She cackled. I sighed. It was going to be a long ride.

As the bus took off and picked up speed, everything started bouncing and squeaking. The familiar sounds reminded me of the poem Tim and I had made up one day on our way to school. How did that go again?

The rhythm on our school bus is really pretty cool.
We bounce and ping and squeak and sing all the way
to school.

Tim and I had to keep ourselves entertained somehow on that almost hour-long ride to school. How would I pass the time now? With Diane squawking beside me, the trip was going to seem like an eternity.

Our bus route was the same as last year. It took us over

lots of skinny country roads. As was my custom, I began praying that we wouldn't meet another car coming the other way on one of those skinny roads. When that happened, Mr. Rockwell had to pull way over to the side of the road, and then the dirt got all stirred up and the bus leaned. I was afraid that one day the bus might topple right over like some big dead bug.

The worst part of the trip was on Jeffers Road. Just before we picked up Russell, we had to go over a skinny bridge. The bridge had high concrete sides that almost came up to the windows of the bus. As we neared the bridge, I thought about my mom trying to thread a needle. If she didn't get it lined up just right, the thread hit the sides of the needle and bent, and she had to keep licking the thread and trying again and again until it finally went through the hole. As the bus approached the bridge, I pictured the bus missing the hole and bending like the thread. So when we made the turn onto Jeffers Road, I always closed my eyes and crossed my fingers and hoped that Mr. Rockwell hadn't had too much coffee that morning so his hands wouldn't shake and he could get that fat bus through the skinny slot.

It was time. I closed my eyes and crossed my fingers. Birdlips began pecking.

"What are you doing? You're supposed to cross your fingers and lift your feet over *railroad* crossings, not bridges. And you don't have to close your eyes, either."

I ignored her and braced myself, clutching the top of the seat in front of me as best I could with my remaining uncrossed two fingers and thumb of each hand. I suddenly had a vision of Birdlips after hitting the bridge, beak crumpled like Woody Woodpecker when he tried to drill into a petrified tree.

"You can stop now, we're over the bridge," Birdlips chirped.

I opened my eyes and relaxed as we approached Russell's house.

Russell. Our poem had a verse about him, too.

> *He makes a stop at Russell's house, then takes off*
> *once again.*
> *Russell staggers to his seat. He'll make it, we know*
> *he can.*

I hadn't thought about Russell all summer. Russell was kind of easy to forget. He was so quiet. I looked at Diane. Suddenly that didn't seem like such a bad thing.

Russell stood at the end of his driveway in baggy jeans

and a wrinkled gray T-shirt. His hair looked choppy, like he had cut it himself. Russell had about a million little brothers and sisters, and a bunch of them were standing in the front yard. A few chickens strutted around, pecking at the dirt. I didn't realize Russell had chickens, too. His chickens looked a lot nicer than ours, though. One of Russell's little sisters was even holding one. She stroked its head and gaped at the big yellow bug that had just swallowed up her brother.

"Seat four, bud," Mr. Rockwell instructed him.

Russell scuffed along the aisle, head down. The old metal lunch box that he carried his marbles in was tucked up under his arm. He slid into the seat behind me without a word. As the bus took off, his marbles rolled and clicked together.

Diane turned in her seat. "Hey, Russell. I'm glad to see you haven't lost your marbles yet." The way she cackled made me wonder if one of Russell's hens had jumped on the bus with him. I gave Russell a sympathetic smile. He rolled his eyes and shook his head.

The bus stopped again and again for kid after kid standing at the end of driveway after driveway. Finally, Neapolis Elementary School appeared, interrupting the steady stream of cornfields flying by my window. Like a starched shirt, the school stood stiff and white at the junction of County Roads 294 and 306, so far out in the country that the roads didn't even have names, just numbers. We lurched into the parking lot, stones crunching, stirring up a cloud of dust. I took a deep breath. Somehow I had managed to survive another white-knuckled bus ride. The bus squealed to a stop and Mr. Rockwell flung open the doors. We all tumbled out and scattered, everyone pairing up with their best friends from last year, which of course left me, like the cheese in "The Farmer in the Dell," standing alone.

As the dust settled, I approached the building. At the bottom of the steps I paused to let the morning sun shine down on me just a little bit longer. I wanted just one more breath of the still-summer air. I knew that once I stepped inside, that was it. Summer was officially over. I took a big breath, held it, counted to five, and then let it out slowly. Head down, I watched Slick and Smooth place themselves firmly on one cement step after another. At the top of the steps my head bumped into something soft. I looked up, then up some more, into the grinning face of the new school janitor.

❏　4

TIGHT FIT

"HEY, TWINKIE, want to see my new office?"

Dad looked proud, poised at the top of the steps in his crisply ironed khaki shirt and pants. There was no sign of the "Green Frog" I had seen earlier.

"You have an office?" Then I remembered the coal room where Lester, the old janitor, used to hang out. I had always been curious about that room. Lester never let anyone down there, especially kids.

"Come on. You still have a few minutes before *I* ring the bell."

I followed him into the school and down the hall. Midway between the girls' and boys' bathrooms stood a heavy steel door. Dad leaned into it, then held it open, making a sweeping motion with his arm for me to enter. When the door clanked shut behind us, all the noise and confusion that was the first day at Neapolis School disappeared. I was in another world. We descended four gray concrete steps into the dark, quiet, warm, cozy cave of the janitor's office.

A small back door stood open and looked out onto the playground. Near that sat a big soft brown chair. There were tools and mops and buckets and cleaning supplies. On the wall next to a calendar hung a layout of the school with exit routes marked in red in case of a fire. I studied the drawing.

Neapolis School had been built as a one-room schoolhouse and was later enlarged, but not by much. The whole school consisted of only three classrooms, the kitchen, the bathrooms, and one big room that served as the cafeteria, art room, gym, and music room. We called it the C.A.G.M. Which is what it felt like they did to us there—cage 'em.

Only three classrooms and five grades meant we had to share. Fourth and fifth grades were lumped together with Ms. Cordle, who did double duty herself as teacher and school principal. Mrs. Bardon ruled the second and third graders, and the first graders got Mrs. Potter all to themselves. They were lucky—not for having Mrs. Potter as a teacher, but for not having to share. It was hard to concentrate on your own work when the teacher only had to take three steps over to reach the other side of the room, where she'd be teaching another class. It was like suffering through two grades at once.

At the end of a long hallway was the kitchen. It was pretty typical except for one magical and wonderful thing, and I don't mean Mrs. Haskins, the cook. In the far corner, hidden behind a trapdoor in the ceiling, was the school bell. All you could see of the bell was the rope. From a small hole cut in the trapdoor, the rope hung thick and prickly, still and lifeless. Until someone pulled it into action. Then what that plain-looking rope could do.

The janitor always rang the bell before and after school, but sometimes Ms. Cordle would choose an after-recess bell ringer from the fourth or fifth grade. Some kids didn't want to be chosen to ring the bell. They were afraid of Mrs. Haskins. But I was always willing to risk getting barked at by her just so I could ring the bell. I was pretty sure she wouldn't bite.

Not just anybody can ring a bell, anyway. Correct bell ringing is a fine art. Since the bell itself can't be seen, hidden as it is behind the trapdoor, the bell ringer has to imagine what position the bell is in at all times. You have to pull hard, but not too hard. If you pull too hard, you could pull the bell right over and then it might get stuck and then you probably wouldn't be picked to ring the bell again. The trick is to pull just until you feel it almost reach the top, then you let the rope run through your hands until the bell swings back down. Then you pull again, hard.

Pull, release, wait. Pull, release, wait.

I bend my knees when I pull. I really get my body into it. Once I have the rhythm down, I can relax and just enjoy the feeling of power, listening to that bell ring out, making everyone run in from recess. I make them quit their games of Four Square and tag and Red Rover. I make them run back inside and sit down in their seats and be quiet. Ha!

When Diane is chosen to ring the bell, she stoops almost to the floor when she pulls. I warned her about that. She pulls too hard. One of these days she's going to pull too far, and the bell is going to go over the top and get stuck. But somehow she always gets away with it. Taking it to the limit, but never going over the top.

"So, what do you think?" Dad brought me back from my daydreams to the coal room.

"Cool," I said, turning in a slow circle to take it all in.

"Actually, it stays pretty warm in here with the furnace and all."

I groaned at Dad's lame joke, but I had to admit I was beginning to warm up to the idea of having Dad here. This could be a nice place for me to come and relax and get away from it all, I thought. A small consolation prize for having to go to school with my dad.

But what would it really be like having my dad at school? Would the other kids tease me because he was just a janitor? Diane's dad traveled a lot. He wore a tie and carried a brief-case. My dad wore a khaki shirt and carried a broom.

Or would they be jealous, thinking I could get away with more stuff because my dad worked at the school?

Would I?

Just then I caught sight of the heavy steel door at the top of the steps, and a strange feeling came over me, like a dark cloud passing in front of the sun. I shivered and hugged my elbows, chilled by the sudden thought of this nice warm cave becoming like that metal tub: cold, gray, and suffocating.

I was beginning to get this funny feeling that having my dad at school was going to be a lot more complicated than I thought.

```
❏  5
R.H.I.P.
```

As FIFTH GRADERS, we got to sit on the side of the room near the windows. "R.H.I.P.," Dad said. "Rank has its privileges."

I slid into the desk where Ms. Cordle had taped a red-construction-paper apple with my name on it. *Penelope* almost didn't fit across the apple. She should have given me a yellow construction-paper banana instead. Or better yet, a yellow construction-paper Twinkie.

I was assigned to the last seat in the row, which suited me just fine.

Even from my new point of view near the windows, the place looked pretty much the same as last year. The same cursive alphabet stretched above the blackboard, the perfectly formed letters looking just a little more yellowed. The blackboard was clean. Of course. Last week Dad had bragged about how shiny "his" floors were, how "his" windows sparkled, how "his" blackboards were spotless, and how the desks were lined up in nice straight rows as if at attention in "his" classrooms. I thought he was taking this job *way* too seriously. I looked down at the wooden strips that made up the floor. They were so shiny they looked wet.

My classmates filed in. Dave Wilson sat in front, rubbing his open palm over the flat top of his new buzz haircut. Across from him sat Linda, wearing a necklace with half a heart that said *Friends*. Audrey sat diagonally from Linda. Her half said *Best*. Across from Audrey was Billy Hill, half of a matching set himself. His twin brother, Bailey, sat in the third row across from Brad. Brad had let his hair grow over the summer, and now a short skinny braid lay limply on his neck. Diane was behind Brad and towered in the seat in front of me. Maybe I could hide behind her when I didn't want Ms. Cordle to call on me. Across from Diane sat Russell, chin in hand.

There were nineteen of us in all, ten fourth graders and nine fifth graders, and most were participating in the required first-day-of-school moaning and groaning about the person they had to sit next to. I looked over at the desk next to me. My stomach clenched. The desk was empty.

Am I supposed to act as if everything is okay? That this is just the way things worked out? With five desks in a row, and now only nine fifth graders, we were one fifth grader short of filling up the two rows. Which left the last seat in the second row, the seat that just happened to be across from mine, very, very empty.

I bit my lip. Would anything ever be normal again? What was normal, anyway? *Normal* was just a six-letter word. *Normal* was one of those words that, if said about ten times over, starts to sound like some alien language, like something you don't understand the meaning of.

Normal, normal, normal, normal, normal, normal, normal, normal, normal, normal. Today my name is Normal.

Not.

If this is normal, normal *s-u-x.*

Just then the bell started clanging. That would be Dad. Everyone quieted down. I pictured Dad in the kitchen, pulling on that thick rope, the muscles in his upper arms tightening, relaxing, the rope running through his callused palms.

Over and over it rang out. *Bong. Bong. Bong.* Out over our heads and over the crows in the cornfields and the cows in the pastures.

Why do schools have bells? Tim would have had an answer.

When the clanging didn't stop after a minute or so, kids

started looking at one another, then giggling. I just shook my head. Dad was having fun now. I knew the feeling. Too much fun to stop. Ms. Cordle cleared her throat then rolled her eyes upward as if willing it to stop. Finally the clanging slowed, along with the giggling, and then it was quiet again.

Audrey was chosen to hold the flag as we all stood and recited the Pledge of Allegiance. As soon as we sat down, Ms. Cordle started taking attendance. She held the thin black book in her hands like a church hymnal, and called out our names, last names first. "Cross, Linda."

Cross Linda and you'll be sorry, I thought.

"Franklin, Brad."

I kind of liked his name better that way. Franklin Brad instead of Brad Franklin.

"Grant, Penelope."

Grant Penelope one wish, please.

"Hill, Bailey."

Everyone cracked up. It sounded like *hillbilly,* but with a southern accent.

"Hill, Billy."

It got worse. Even Hill, Billy and Hill, Bailey laughed. Ms. Cordle gave us all a "grow up" look.

I shrank down behind my Diane shield. At least Birdlips

was good for something. I peeked over Diane's shoulder and studied Ms. Cordle as she made her way down the list of students. She loomed large and scary as ever at the front of the room like the giant in "Jack and the Beanstalk." Her thick glasses made her pupils look like billiard balls, even from the last seat in the row. She slicked her short gray hair back like a man and rotated the three dresses she owned. They were all the same short-sleeved, belt-at-the-waist, long-flowing-skirt style, just different colors. Today was blue day. She kept a handkerchief tucked into the strap of her bra and used it often. For half of the day, she would stand, feet planted shoulder width apart, arms crossed, at the front of the room. She'd stay there until it was time to take three steps over and plant her feet and cross her arms in front of the fourth grade. She'd rub her thumbs and index fingers together constantly in that crossed-arm position, as if rolling little spitballs.

I jumped when Ms. Cordle snapped her attendance book shut, satisfied that all were present and accounted for. All but one, that is.

As if reading my mind, Ms. Cordle cleared her throat. "Boys and girls," she began. She looked at her feet, then back up at us, and adjusted her glasses. "I'm sure by now you have all heard the sad news that your classmate Tim Daniels passed away this summer."

Passed away. Tim would have snorted at that phrase. Why doesn't she just say it? He died, okay? He didn't pass away, move on, buy the farm, or kick the bucket. He died.

Ms. Cordle continued. "Obviously our class won't be the same without him." She took a deep breath. "But I think Tim would have wanted us to carry on"—she lifted her chin—"full speed ahead." Her lips tightened and she nodded, as if trying to convince herself of this. "So, let's get started, shall we?"

That was Ms. Cordle. Get right down to business. No chitchat about how we all spent our wonderful carefree summer vacations. Too bad. I could have entertained everyone with tales from Poetry Therapy.

Poetry Therapy. It *was* like a fairy tale. I never did believe it was really going to work. But I tried to keep up the part about naming my feelings anyway, hoping that one day I'd hit upon some magic word or maybe some magic phrase that would make everything normal again so I wouldn't have to put up with those prickly Tim memories anymore. I looked again at the empty seat. I named it Black Hole.

"I'll be spending the better part of the morning distributing textbooks," Ms. Cordle was saying. "I would appreciate your full cooperation."

Aye, aye, Captain. Full speed ahead.

The process of handing out textbooks was always a long, boring one. Ms. Cordle called us up in alphabetical order and wrote *new* or *good* or *fair* or *poor* on the inside cover of the book next to our name so she could see how badly we were beating them up over the course of the school year. Her desk was piled high with stacks of books. She kept her head down, concentrating on accurately judging the quality of each book. Naturally, everyone took advantage of the situation.

Audrey passed a note to Linda. Dave looked at me, grinned and wriggled his eyebrows, then slipped a note to Brad. Hill, Billy and Hill, Bailey didn't need to write notes. They could read each other's minds. I looked over at the empty desk beside me. If Tim were sitting there in that seat like he was supposed to be, he'd be handing me a note right about now, too. Then I got an idea. I pulled the pink pad out of my pocket again. I'd show them. I could write notes, too.

FOR Tim   URGENT ☒

FROM Me
_____

MESSAGE This is going to be one long school year. Miss
Cordle is the same as ever, and I think Dave Wilson STILL has

---

a crush on me. Now that you're not hanging around with me all the time, I'm afraid he's going to try to make his move. I wish I had paid more attention last year when you tried to teach me those karate kicks.

By the time I had finished my note, Franklin, Brad was on his way back to his desk with his new geography book. Dave stuck out his foot, but Brad just stepped high and laughed, not even looking back at Dave.

I folded my note into fourths and pressed it into the palm of my hand. When Ms. Cordle called "Grant, Penelope," I stood and slid the note into the belly of the empty desk beside me, then walked up front to grab my fifth-grade dose of oceans, deserts, plateaus, and grasslands.

The morning dragged on. Ms. Cordle called out names for math books, then English books, then history books. Finally, she let us out for recess. I headed straight for the shade of the oak tree and sat, leaning against its large trunk. Tim and I had spent many a recess here under this oak tree, making roads and playing with his Matchbox cars. I watched my classmates. Even though it was hot, everyone ran around like chickens with their heads cut off, and I certainly knew what that looked like. Once a month or so, Dad would get a craving for a Sunday dinner of fried chicken. He'd chase down a couple of chickens, grab them by the legs, throw them over an old tree stump, and whack off their heads with an ax. Then he'd let go and they'd take off, headless, running all willy-nilly around the yard. The chickens only lasted a few seconds without their heads before keeling over, but it seemed like forever. The whole awful scene was like something out of a bad horror movie.

I picked up a rock and began drawing headless chickens in the dirt. Why didn't Dad ever grab Ares, that nasty old rooster, and whack his head off? Ares was probably way too tough to eat, and for sure too rotten.

"Wanna play marbles?"

I looked up. Russell peered down at me through his long, choppy bangs, marble tin under his arm. I hadn't recognized his voice. He sounded different somehow.

"No thanks," I said, then noticed that Russell was staring at my drawings of headless chickens. I quickly erased them with my palm.

"Hey, Chief, I'll play." Russell and I both looked up at the sound of a very familiar voice. Dad. Of course. Recess monitor was one of his duties as janitor. I was about to tell him that Lester had always just watched us from the top steps of the building, but it was too late. Dad was already following Russell to the blacktop. He sat down cross-legged on the pavement. Russell knelt, pulled a piece of pale blue chalk out of his marble tin, and drew a circle. For a second I had a vision of Tim sitting there cross-legged, playing marbles with Russell. I shook my head like an Etch A Sketch to erase the image. Before long, Billy and Bailey ran up and joined the game. The marbles clicked, followed by either a groan or a whoop.

I leaned back against the tree. Today my name is Lone Ranger.

❏ 6
PULLING STRINGS

FANS BUZZED, one on each side of the room, whirring close, humming away, whirring close again. The edges of my history book fluttered with each pass. Ms. Cordle stood on the fourth grade side of the room, reviewing multiplication tables. We were supposed to be reading Chapter One in our history books. I was having a hard time keeping all the numbers straight. I was reading about 1776, yet hearing the hypnotic chant of the fourth graders: "Seven times six is forty-two, seven times seven is forty-nine, seven times eight . . ."

I gave up and decided to write another note to Tim. It felt good to be writing to him. With the *While You Were Out* notes, I could pretend he was only out for the day, just like the message pad said.

By the time I finished the note, Ms. Cordle was passing out a worksheet to the fourth graders. I quickly folded the note, then leaned over and shoved it into the empty desk just before Ms. Cordle clomped back over to our side of the room.

"I would like to see how many of last year's spelling words this class has retained over the summer," Ms. Cordle began. "Take out a piece of paper and a pencil and number from one to twenty, skipping lines."

Groans. Whispers. Coughs. Three-ring binders snapped open, clapped shut. Pencils rapped. Toes tapped.

Spelling was one of my better subjects. Maybe I didn't know a thing about when or where or what the Revolutionary War was, but at least I could spell it. I glanced at Dave, who was already looking at me. His flattop glistened with sweat. He winked. I rolled my eyes.

Each year when we had our annual Boys vs. Girls spelling bee, Tim and I were always the last two standing. I usually choked. I even remembered the word from our last spelling bee that had tripped me up. *Restaurant.* I could never re-member where to put the *u.* Now, with Tim gone, Dave obviously thought he'd be the boy to beat. Fat chance. But Dave was tricky. If there was a way to cheat in spelling, Dave would be the one to figure it out.

I glanced at Russell. His jaws were clenched and he had a firm grip on his No. 2 pencil. Tim used to drill Russell on the bus before a big spelling test. Russell hated spelling tests.

Ms. Cordle, on the other hand, loved spelling tests. They gave her an opportunity to enunciate even more than she normally did. She said each word so precisely, her lips still formed the last syllable even after we had finished writing it down. She began firing some fourth-grade words at us.

"Num-ber one: *fetch.* Please fetch a pail of water. Fetch."

Piece of cake. I wrote it down and looked up. Ms. Cordle's lips still formed a rectangle from the *ch* sound.

"Num-ber two: *meadow.* The cows are in the meadow. Meadow."

There were those cows again. Ms. Cordle always gave the word, made a sentence, then repeated the word. It drove me nuts. I looked around the room. Russell was already erasing. His desk jiggled and creaked as he rubbed furiously with his huge pink eraser that said, *I never make BIG mistakes.*

I zipped through *bargain* and *greet* and *speech.*

"Num-ber six," Ms. Cordle continued, "*fleet.* To run fast is to be fleet of foot. Fleet."

I wrote it down. I'd like to be fleet of foot right out the door, I thought, tapping my pencil. Maybe I could pretend it needed sharpening. The pencil sharpener was on the wall right next to the door. I imagined myself cranking the handle, my courage building inside of me with every turn, then making a run for freedom. Zip! Fleet of foot right out the door.

"Num-ber seven," Ms. Cordle interrupted my thoughts of escape with another spelling word. "*Odor.* What is that strange odor? Odor."

I wrote it down. No problem. Were these actually fourth-grade words? I glanced at the fourth graders sitting with their heads down, scratching out answers on a math paper. They should be paying attention to these spelling words. They'd probably be getting this same quiz in about ten minutes.

Dave raised his hand. "Would you repeat that please, Ms. Cordle?"

"Odor," she repeated.

Come on, I thought, let's get this over with.

Dave shook his head. "Sorry, once more?"

I almost groaned out loud. Dave was such a pain.

"ODOR." Ms. Cordle leaned forward, clutching the spelling book to her chest, directing the word at Dave, practically hurling it at him.

Diane snorted. Linda looked down at her paper and shaded her eyes to hide the smirk on her face. Audrey was biting the end of her pencil and sitting on the edge of her chair. No one dared make a sound. Dave stuck his little finger in his ear and wriggled it furiously. "Did you say 'ogre'?"

"ODOR!" Ms. Cordle spat. "O-d-o-r!"

"Thank you," said Dave, writing down the word.

Everyone burst out laughing. Ms. Cordle, red in the face, adjusted her glasses and quickly scanned the room, watching pencils. I glanced down at my paper.

Number seven. Oder. O-d-e-r.

I looked back at Ms. Cordle, then back down at my paper. I felt myself getting hot all over. Ms. Cordle dictated two more words. I wrote them down without thinking about anything but my mistake. If I left it wrong, I would look pretty stupid for not taking advantage of a "gimme." If I changed it, was that cheating? I wasn't sure.

Criminy cupcakes, she had given us the answer!

I was sure Tim was up in heaven. If I ever wanted to see him again, I had to be really good. If I corrected my mistake, would that be enough to keep me out of heaven? Enough to keep me from ever seeing Tim again?

I looked again at the empty seat beside me. How I wished that Tim were still sitting there. He'd know. He was always good at figuring out those fuzzy gray areas. Maybe Tim could pull some strings for me. Maybe he could say, "Listen God, she's a friend of mine. Give her a break, okay?" He'd do that for me.

I waited until Ms. Cordle had dictated two more words before I furtively, but thoroughly, erased the *e* and replaced it with an *o*.

I SAT DOWN in the cafeteria, still thinking about that spelling test. Would Ms. Cordle notice the eraser marks on number seven when she got to my paper? When Dave walked by carrying his lunch tray, I narrowed my eyes to tiny slits and glared at him. If I didn't get to heaven because I cheated on a spelling test, it was all Dave's fault.

I opened my lunch box. No surprises there. Peanut-butter-and-jelly, an apple, and two cookies. I was just unwrapping the wax paper when who should sit down across from me but Dad. I was so shocked I couldn't speak. I heard giggles from down the bench.

"Mind if I join you?" he asked, already sitting down.

"Aren't you supposed to sit with the teachers?" I asked in a raspy whisper.

"I'd rather spend some time with my favorite student," he

said. "Besides, what better way to carry out my duties as lunch monitor than to get right down here on the front lines?

"Hey, Chief, nice game today," Dad called when Russell walked by.

"Thanks," Russell said over his shoulder as he headed for an empty spot next to Hill, Billy and Hill, Bailey. Russell acted as if it were perfectly natural for the school janitor to be sitting with the kids. Then Birdlips flew in and landed next to me. Of course she wasn't going to let it slide.

"What are you doing here, Mr. Grant?"

"I'm having lunch with Pretty Penelope Rose," he sang.

I slumped and considered sliding right on under the table. Diane laughed. "You're so funny, Mr. Grant."

Dad opened his huge black metal lunch box with a clang that echoed off the cafeteria walls. He removed his thermos, smiling and nodding at every single kid who walked by. I was afraid I was going to be sick. When he unwrapped his sandwich, I was *sure* I was going to be sick.

He eagerly took a huge bite and instantly the aroma of onion rose like someone had dropped a stink bomb. "Ewwwwww's" and "pee-yous" ran up one side of the table and down the other like the Wave at a ball game. Some kids pinched their nostrils shut.

"What are you eating?" Diane asked, wrinkling her nose.

"Peanut-butter-and-onion," Dad said, his mouth full of it. "S'great. Wanna bite?" He extended his sandwich across the table to her. Diane leaned so far back I thought she'd fall off the bench.

"Ah, no thanks," she said. "I think I see Linda over there." She grabbed her tray and was gone. Perfect.

Dad shrugged. "No accounting for tastes," he said.

"What's wrong with peanut-butter-and-jelly?" I asked, waving my sandwich under his nose. Other than the fact that it doesn't repel birds of prey, I thought as I watched Diane land at another table.

Dad pushed it away. "Bor-r-r-ing. I need something with a little zing."

I sat up straight and tried to peek over the edge of the monster lunch box. "You don't have any more of those in there, do you?"

"Nope," he said. "But I've got something even better." He pulled another sandwich from the depths and held it up. "Smashed bean." He winked.

My spine went limp and I slunk down again. We had had bean soup for supper last night. My creative recycling dad never missed a chance to get more mileage out of a meal. I studied my father as he chewed happily on his smashed-bean sandwich. His thick fingers held it firmly, causing globs of smashed beans to drip out onto the table. Finally, he finished his sandwich and scoured the bottom of his lunch pail for more food.

The Hill twins hustled back toward the kitchen to deposit their trays. Most of the boys inhaled their lunches so they could get out to recess sooner. Russell followed, his marble tin shoved up under his armpit.

"Hey, Chief, looks like you're in need of a little repair work there," Dad said, nodding at Russell's tin. "Mind if I take a look?"

Russell stopped, shrugged, then handed over the box. "It used to be my lunch box," he explained. "I guess it got a little too heavy when I started carrying marbles in there." Russell shoved his hands in his pockets and watched as Dad examined it.

"Looks like it just needs a new clip. I think I might have something in my office that will work. Can you leave this with me until after school?"

"Sure," Russell said, backing away. "See ya then."

What will he do at recess without his marbles? I wondered.

Dad smiled. "Today my name is Mr. Fix-it. Your teacher wants me to fix the latch on the window in your classroom, too. I'll do that after recess."

"Why do you call him 'Chief'?" I asked.

"Huh? Oh, you mean Russ? Well, have you ever heard the old saying 'Still waters run deep'?"

I shook my head.

"It means that sometimes calm, quiet people like Russ have deep thoughts and feelings. So, whenever I see him I think 'still waters,' and that sounds to me like the name of an Indian chief. Chief Still Waters. So I just call him Chief for short."

"Wow, pretty deep yourself there, Dad," I said.

"Thank you." He turned his attention back to his lunch box, ignoring my sarcasm. He rummaged around, then pulled out a prune and held it up between his thumb and index finger. "Looks kind of pitiful, doesn't it? All shriveled up like it wants to disappear. I think I'll save it for later. I've got to get back to work. Playground monitor, you know. Tough job, but somebody's got to do it." He took one last loud slurp of his coffee, then packed up and left.

I watched him as he made his way out of the cafeteria, nodding and smiling to every single person he passed on the way.

I sighed. Today my name is Shriveled Prune.

❏ 8
DOOMED

AFTER LUNCH I sat on the swing in the school yard, lazily pushing myself back and forth. I could hear the *slap, slap* of the jump rope on the pavement as Linda and Diane twirled and a long line of girls waited their turns to jump. Russell, temporarily marbleless, stood on the basketball court playing pig with Hill, Billy and Hill, Bailey. The rest of the boys played tackle tag behind me. I didn't even have to look. I could hear the thumps and grunts coming from the open field. I pulled out the pink pad.

FOR Tim   URGENT ❏

FROM Me

MESSAGE They make me sick. The same games every day.
You and I used to think up new things to do all the time. The

> days you brought your Matchbox cars were the days I wished recess would never end. Now I wish we wouldn't have recess.

I slid the pad back into my pocket, then felt a sudden jerk from behind me. I clutched the chains of the swing and tried to turn around, but I was up in the air before I could see who was behind me. Looking down, I saw the top of my father's head emerge from under the swing. He had given me an underdoggie! That whole field of boys behind me could probably see my underwear. I tried to tuck my jeans skirt under my leg with one hand while I held on tight with the other. I wondered if Dad could tell how mad I was, but my face was probably a blur. He laughed and walked away.

As the swing slowed, I dragged my feet in the dirt. The dust flew up and coated my socks. I kept an eye on Dad as he wandered over to the girls jumping rope. He stopped, then rolled up his sleeves. Oh no. He wouldn't.

He did. He got in line. I closed my eyes. When I heard the squeals I opened them. He was actually doing it. Jumping rope. The change jingled in his pants pocket and his feet thumped the ground. The girls chanted.

"TEDDY BEAR, TEDDY BEAR, TURN AROUND."

Oh no, not that one. He's going to break his neck.

"TEDDY BEAR, TEDDY BEAR, TOUCH THE GROUND."

The girls laughed so hard they had trouble getting the words out.

"TEDDY BEAR, TEDDY BEAR, TURN OUT THE LIGHT.

TEDDY BEAR, TEDDY BEAR, SAY GOOD NIGHT."

Dad caught himself in the rope when he tried to move out. By this time the girls were bent in half laughing. Some of the little ones were actually rolling in the grass. I eyed the cornfield surrounding the playground. How long would it take before anybody missed me?

When I looked back, Dad was wiping his forehead with a handkerchief. He glanced at his watch, then pranced up the steps of the school to ring the bell.

As the lonely sound of the bell pealed out, everyone ran inside. I just sat and listened. The bell seemed to be chanting, "Doomed, doomed, doomed."

IN HISTORY CLASS, I stared out the window and thought about Dad. How could I get him to behave? I pulled out the pink pad.

FOR Tim   URGENT ❏

FROM Me

MESSAGE I think my dad's trying to be my friend-for-now until I make a new friend-for-keeps. Nobody understands. You'll always be my friend-for-keeps.

Ms. Cordle's voice floated over me as she rambled on about Ohio becoming a state. The door creaked open behind me. I quickly shoved the pink pad inside my desk. Ms. Cordle nodded to the visitor and went on.

"In 1803 . . ."

Who had come in? Trying to find out without being caught turning around in my seat, I turned my head slightly, then rolled my eyes sideways as far as they would go. My nose blocked half my view. Sometimes a school-board member or a supervisor would slink in and lurk at the back of the room, observing the class. I guess they wanted to make sure Ms. Cordle was teaching us the stuff she was supposed to and not witchcraft or something, although Ms. Cordle would certainly be qualified.

They usually didn't come in this early in the school year, though. Finally, unable to withstand the suspense any longer, I turned around in my seat, then clapped my hand over my mouth. Dad again! Like a balloon losing air, complete with the little squeaky sound, I slid down and around in my seat.

Ms. Cordle droned on. "And so, in 1803, Ohio became a state, making the total number of states now . . . ?" She left it open as if we were supposed to fill in the blank. She peered over her glasses at the class. No hands went up. The only sound in the room was the clinking and clunking noises Dad was making as he pawed through his toolbox, looking for something to fix the window with.

"Anyone?" Ms. Cordle persisted.

The next sound in the room was the only sound I hoped *not* to hear.

"Pssst, Penny." I didn't bother to turn around. Without even looking, I could picture Dad behind me, screwdriver in one hand, the other hand beside his mouth as if whispering, even though I was certain the bus drivers idling out in the parking lot could hear his raspy voice.

"Seventeen. Say seventeen."

I turned around, hoping to force him to shut up just by the sourness of my glare. When Ms. Cordle spotted him, he quickly turned back to the window as if innocent. He didn't fool Ms. Cordle, though. She doesn't miss much.

"Mr. Grant. Since no one else in the class seems to know the answer to the question, why don't you help us out?"

For once, he was embarrassed instead of me. Little round blotches of pink spread out over his cheekbones like red Kool-Aid spilling onto the kitchen floor. For a minute I actually felt sorry for him. I knew what it was like to be caught off guard by Ms. Cordle. I held my breath.

"Ah, it was the seventeenth," Dad said quietly. "Ohio was the seventeenth state to enter the union."

"Correct. Thank you, Mr. Grant."

I let the breath out.

"Ohio wanted to become a state in 1800," he continued, speaking louder and faster, "but they didn't have enough people yet."

I caught my breath again. I couldn't believe it. He was like a train engine, picking up speed as he chugged along.

The rest of the class had turned around in their seats to watch Dad spout off. Dave was nodding and rubbing his chin like some wise old professor. Audrey's mouth just hung open in a little O of disbelief. Birdlips put her braid under her nose like a mustache and held it there by curling her top lip. None of this fazed Dad in the least. He chugged on.

"You see, a territory needed at least sixty thousand people to become a state, and Ohio was a tad short in 1800."

I groaned and slid lower in my seat. I just wanted to go home, but I wanted to be whisked there magically like Dorothy in *The Wizard of Oz*. I tapped my heels together three times and chanted under my breath, "There's no place like home. There's no place like home." I sighed. Without the ruby slippers I was doomed. The bus ride home would be brutal.

Finally, Dad ran out of his little-known, little-cared-about facts on Ohio, fixed the window, and left the room. Ms. Cordle squeezed in a homework assignment just as the bell rang out for the last time that day. Dad again. At least when he was ringing the bell I knew where he was and that he was staying out of trouble. Too bad I couldn't put that bell around his neck, like a cow.

I grabbed my book bag, kept my head down, and scurried for the door like a frightened mole. Sprinting to the bus, I burrowed into my seat, but only managed to postpone the inevitable.

One by one my classmates filed by me to take their seats.

Linda: "What's for lunch tomorrow, Penelope? Sardines? Remind me to bring my nose plugs."

Dave: "Your face was a nice shade of purple when your dad gave you that underdoggie. Tomorrow is he going to teeter-totter with you?"

Birdlips: "Hey, can I come over tonight and have your dad do my history homework?"

Everybody laughed. Except Russell. He slid into the seat behind me, leaned forward, and practically whispered in my ear. "Your dad fixed my marble box."

"Yeah, just call him Mr. Fix-it," I mumbled over my shoulder.

"Maybe he can teach me some stuff," Russell said, as if talking to himself.

The bus lurched into gear. I stared out the window as the bus picked up speed and roared away from Neapolis School.

A hot breeze blew my bangs off my forehead as cornfields flew by in a blur. When we rounded the bend on Miller Road, I remembered how Tim would grab my elbow at that curve to keep from falling off the seat. Another verse from our poem came back to me.

> Up and down the hills we go, around the curves we
> weave.
> We lean to the left, then the right, through orange
> and yellow leaves.

When the bus approached my house, I didn't even wait for it to come to a complete stop before I moved toward the door, staggering like my uncle Neal after he's been drinking beer. I remembered another verse.

> Russell wobbles, grips his lunch box firmly in his hand.
> Bang! Bang! It hits the seats. That's our school-bus band.

Well, thanks to Mr. Fix-it, Russell can bang his lunch/ marble box against the seats again. When the bus released me, I ran as fast as I could to the house. I slammed the door and pulled out the *While You Were Out* pad. I sank down at the dining-room table and wrote a note to Mom.

FOR Mom   URGENT ☒

FROM P.   R.   G.

Pretty Rotten Grade (5th)

_____

MESSAGE I think I'm coming down with something. My
stomach feels all shriveled up like the prunes in Dad's lunch—
pits included! I might have to stay home with you tomorrow.

I LAY IN BED and stared at the glow-in-the-dark constellation on my ceiling. Tim had told me about the Belt of Orion. It was easy to make and only used up three stars. The clock ticked slowly on the nightstand. Maybe if I wound it tighter, time would go by quicker. Just then the door creaked open and a stream of light from the hallway spread across my bedroom floor.

"Psst. You still awake?"

Mom crossed the room and lowered herself gently onto the edge of my bed. "I had a feeling you weren't asleep. I read your note. Rough day, huh?"

Rough was not exactly the word I had in mind to describe my first day of school. *Agonizing* might be closer. *Brutal* maybe. *Torture* better yet. But I didn't want to tell her that it was so bad I was writing notes to empty desks. Mom didn't wait for an answer anyway. "And how was it having your father there?"

I would have told her how I felt about Dad being the janitor if I knew myself. I felt confused about it, dizzy almost, and not just from the underdoggie he had given me at recess. I was glad he finally had a steady job, but every time I turned around, there he was.

"Your dad's pretty proud of himself for landing that job," Mom said. "You know how hard it is for him to stick with one thing for any length of time. If he can't turn everything into some type of creative project, he loses interest."

How well I knew. "He fixed the handle on Russell's marble box today," I offered, "and the window at the back of my room."

"Well, that's good," she said. "Maybe little projects like that will satisfy his creative streak. Just so he doesn't get too carried away."

She nodded toward my wall. "Can you imagine the look on Ms. Cordle's face if she came in one morning to cows painted on her classroom walls?"

I laughed. It felt good to laugh. It seemed like a million years since I had laughed. It was almost as if my mouth didn't know how to go in that direction anymore.

"He *did* get a little carried away with his lunch, though,"

I said. "Mom, *please* don't let him pack another smashed-bean sandwich."

She laughed. "Don't worry. I went to the grocery store this morning and stocked up on plenty of plain old bologna."

"No onions?"

"No onions."

"But he needs something with a little zing," I said.

Mom sighed. "That he does." She looked thoughtful. "How about a little Dijon mustard? Would that do it, you think?"

"Okay," I said. "But not so much that it drips off the sandwich."

"Deal," she said. Mom bent down, put her arms around me, and squeezed. "You are a brave girl, Penelope Grant."

I squeezed back, tighter.

"And strong," she added.

"Today my name is Boa Constrictor," I said.

"Well, my little Boa, you'd better get some sleep." Mom kissed my cheek and tucked the sheet up under my chin. "I hope you feel better in the morning." She glanced at the clock. "*Later* in the morning, that is."

Then she was gone, our ships completing their pass in the night. I thought about what she had said. I didn't really feel strong at all. And definitely not brave. But I did feel better after the hug.

I rolled my head to the window. I could see at least a million stars, not counting the three on my ceiling. I quickly spotted the brightest star and named it Bright Bead, Tim's star.

"I'll write you again tomorrow," I whispered.

Tim's star winked. "Please do."

SITUATIONAL ANXIETY

THE NEXT MORNING, I had to read the note Mom left for me on the kitchen table twice before it sank in.

FOR *Boa C.*   URGENT ❏

FROM *Mom*

MESSAGE *I think your stomachache might be due to situational anxiety, but just to be safe, skip the Cocoa Puffs. Try dry toast instead.*
  I hope you feel better.
  Today my name is . . .
Dr. Mom   ☺

My stomach felt pruney all morning, even without the Cocoa Puffs. This day was turning out to be the Pits—prune pits—which has got to be worse than cherry pits or armpits or any other kind of pits. By math class, my stomach felt like it was on a roller coaster all by itself. And a ride is no fun if you can't get off.

My mouth watered. I swallowed. Try to think of something calm, soothing, I told myself. Cream of Wheat. Chicken noodle soup. Still waters.

My stomach churned even more. No good. Thinking about food was not good. Okay, I told my stomach, I'm lying in the hammock in the backyard on a nice day.

I wiped sweat off my forehead. *Try again,* my stomach said.

A soft, cool breeze is blowing.

The hammock is swaying too much! Get off! yelled my stomach.

Okay, I'm on my bed, my nice sturdy bed. Alone in my room. It's quiet. I swallowed again; my mouth was watering even more now. I was hot all over. I laid my head down on my desk.

This is not working. My stomach was getting impatient now.

I'm not going to throw up. I feel fine. This will be over in a minute. I *will not* throw up.

My stomach clenched like an angry fist. *Oh yeah?*

I lifted my head, looked around. I've got to get out of here. I raised my hand. Ms. Cordle had her back turned, writing math problems on the board. No time. No time to wait for permission.

Get to the bathroom. Hurry up! my stomach ordered.

I stood up. The room swayed. I grabbed on to my desk. I'm not going to make it. Maybe I can try for the window. But it wasn't open. How well did Dad fix the latch? Would it open easily?

No time. Get out. I lurched toward the door. Swallow. Swallow. Keep it down. Keep it down. At least get out into the hallway.

URP! BLEAH! SPLAT!

"Eww-w-w-w-w-w." The class reacted in unison.

I stared down at the puddle I had made on Dad's shiny floor. From somewhere far away, Ms. Cordle's voice: "Penelope? Are you all right?"

I thought I had made it perfectly clear that I was not. But I wasn't about to stand around and answer questions, or be gawked at by my classmates. I sidestepped the puddle and racewalked down the hall, wanting to run. Away. As far as I could.

But as far as I could get was the coal room. As I made my way there, guiding myself with one hand on the cool, smooth tiles of the hallway walls, I suddenly felt sorry for Dad.

What a horrible job he had—cleaning up kids' puke—even if it was his own kid.

I threw my shoulder into the heavy door that separated the coal room from the rest of the world. I felt weak, but managed to crack it open just enough to squeeze through. I slid my hand along the rail, feeling the grit collect on my palm as I scuffed down the four steps into the school's warm belly.

Dad stood by the open door, gazing out at the fields while he puffed his cigarette. His dark form, silhouetted against the bright outdoors, turned when he heard my steps.

"Well, look what the cat dragged in," he said. "What's up?"

When I got close enough for him to get a good look at me, he figured it out.

"Whoa, you don't look so good. Wait, don't tell me. Today your name is Green Around the Gills."

"I threw up. Right in front of the whole class. I tried to make it to the door, but it was just a few feet too far." I sank into the overstuffed chair and laid my head on its soft fat arm. "You'd better go throw some of that pine stuff on it before the whole class starts puking."

Dad placed his palm gently on my forehead.

"Want to go home?"

I thought for a second. Mom was still home, at least for a while, but she was the one who'd made me come to school today in the first place. "Situational anxiety," huh? I guess I pretty much blew chunks all over "Dr. Mom's" theory. And I did feel better just being in this almost secret hideaway. It was the lowest spot in the school. Somehow that felt like the perfect place for me to be. So no, I didn't want to go home. But since I couldn't shake my head no very well in the position I was in, with my head lying on the arm of the chair, I just moved my eyes left and right as if paralyzed. Dad covered me with his coat and grabbed a bucket. "I'll be right back," he said. "You just rest."

When he had gone, I lifted my head and looked around the room. This was Dad's kingdom. The overstuffed chair I sat in was his throne. The push broom he had grabbed to sweep up my puke was his scepter. The heavy metal door was like a drawbridge that separated him from his subjects: the teachers, armored knights fighting the little battles in the classrooms; the students, peasants, small nobodies herded silently from place to place. The royal document proclaiming his authority, his boiler's license, hung on the wall. He had told me it was kind of like a diploma saying it was okay for him to run the furnace at school.

Also on the wall was a calendar with a picture of a lake surrounded by pine trees. A canoe was tied to the shore. If Dad really were king of Neapolis School, he would send out a decree that every nice day be declared a holiday and that the whole school should go fishing.

The back door to the coal room stood open and looked out over the playground, the cornfields, my oak tree. This job would be great. Hanging out down here, tending the furnace, not having to deal with kids who laughed at you. I could stay down here all day, all week, all year even. I'd act like a bear and not come out until spring.

No one could bug me here. No Ms. Cordle. No grades. No dates of wars to learn. No names of who fought whom and where and why. Down here I could just rest and think. Or *not* think if I felt like it. I shut my eyes and lay back. This was more like it. Maybe if I could come down here every day, school wouldn't be so bad after all.

I must have dozed off because the next thing I knew, Dad was standing over me again.

"How do you feel now?" he asked.

"Better," I said, then quickly added, "but just a little." I didn't want him getting any crazy ideas about sending me back to class.

"If I take you out to the lake, you won't feed the fish, will you? You know they won't take the bait if you give them free food."

Suddenly I really did feel better. I pushed on the arms of the chair and straightened myself. I loved to fish with him.

"I'll be fine," I said. "I think the fresh air will do me good."

"Then it's a date," he said. "As soon as school's out, we'll go."

Finally the bell rang out, ending another school day. I listened while everyone shuffled noisily out of the building. Ms. Cordle would be in the parking lot, making sure everyone got on the buses safely, so I decided it was safe for me to go back to my classroom and grab my book bag.

My classroom was empty and quiet. I paused in the doorway and searched the floor for any sign of my "accident." There was none. Dad had done his job well. I stepped over the threshold. It felt weird being in this room alone. With no one else around, even with the bright fluorescent lights turned off, things I hadn't noticed before seemed to pop out at me.

The watercolors we painted in art class of Christopher Columbus's voyage were taped to the far wall. The fourth grade had made mobiles of oak leaves and acorns that now hung from the light fixtures. I glanced over at the bookshelves running beneath the windows. They were full of books, thick and thin, squeezed tight against one another. This was our library.

Finally, my eyes came to rest on the shoebox. It sat on top of the bookshelf near the pencil sharpener at the back of the room. Tim's pencil collection. He had decorated the box with baseball cards and given it to Ms. Cordle on the final day of school last spring. He was getting very thin by then, almost like a pencil himself. I remembered he had worn his red Cleveland Indians baseball hat that day. It was autographed by Omar Vizquel. Tim didn't have any hair left by then because of the medicine he was taking, so Ms. Cordle allowed him to wear the baseball cap. He had another cap that said CANCER SUCKS, but he couldn't wear that one to school.

So, thin and bald under his red baseball cap, Tim handed over the shoebox filled with hundreds of pencils of different colors and sizes that he had collected. Ms. Cordle had insisted he keep them, saying he would need them again in the fall, but Tim knew better.

After presenting his pencil collection that day, Tim turned around to go back to his seat. That's when I saw Ms. Cordle pull her handkerchief from her bra strap, lift her glasses, and dab her eyes. It was a good thing Tim hadn't seen that. He didn't want anybody feeling sorry for him.

I walked over to the baseball-card-covered shoebox,

lifted the lid, and chose a nice green pencil from Tim's collection. I went back to my desk, sat down, and pulled out the pink pad. In Poetry Therapy they told us about odes. Odes were poems written to one specific person. I clenched the green pencil and wrote.

For Tim	Urgent ❏
From Me	

Message

Ode to a Long Lost Friend

If you only knew

what a line or two

from you

could do

P.

LUCKILY THE LAKE wasn't far from school. I lay on my stomach on the backseat of the station wagon and watched the road whiz by through the ragged, rusty hole in the floor. I knew we were getting close to the lake when the asphalt changed to stone, then dirt.

"Here we are," Dad announced.

I slid out of the car and took a deep breath. The faint smell of pine in the damp lake air made me feel better already. I loved the sounds here, too: the *slop, slop* of the waves as they bumped into the shore, the *caw, caw* of the birds, the *whish* of the wind through the trees, and nothing more.

I followed Dad as he stepped high through overgrown weeds surrounding the lake. Finally we came to his favorite spot: a clearing where he knew the fish were biting and the view was scenic. A long piece of driftwood provided a seat for Dad and a backrest for me.

"Beautiful here, isn't it?" Dad scanned our surroundings. "Look how the light reflects off the waves," he said, pointing. "And check out that line of maples on the shore over there. The leaves are going to be amazing in a couple more weeks. I'll have to come back with my oil paints."

I watched him pull a fat squirming night crawler out of the bait box. I swallowed and reached into my pocket for one of the individually wrapped packets of saltines that Dad had managed to sneak out of Mrs. Haskins's kitchen. I nibbled my cracker and looked out across the lake to where Dad had pointed, but I wasn't really interested in how the sun or the trees looked. I had already decided that this fishing trip would be a good time to talk to Dad about his behavior at school. And what better way to break the ice than good old Poetry Therapy? If it didn't work this time, I was giving up on it for good.

I took a deep breath. "Today my name is Trade Me Places," I began.

"What's that?" Dad asked absently, already deep into his fishing mode.

"Poetry Therapy, Dad. Get with the program."

"Oh yeah, Poetry Therapy. Okay, what's your name again?"

"Trade Me Places," I repeated, slower and louder. "It seems like you'd rather be in class or on the playground with the kids, and I'd rather be alone in the coal room, so let's switch."

He was quiet for a minute, as if he were actually considering it.

"Dad?"

"Today my name is Stuck in a Rut," he announced glumly.

I wrinkled my brow. "What do you mean?"

Dad jabbed his hook into the worm. The look on his face made me wonder if he had jabbed the hook into his finger instead. "This job—" He shrugged.

"I thought you liked this job," I interrupted. "I remember when you first found out you got it. You took Mom and me out to Yawberg's. You let me order the fried shrimp basket and said I could have all the orange pop I wanted."

"Yeah, I did like the job at first. During the summer when no one was around, I spent my time painting walls, polishing floors, patching things up—creative stuff. I'd tune the radio to my favorite station; you know the one that plays 'all oldies, all the time'? And I'd broadcast it over the intercom so that no matter which room I was working in, I could hear it." He sighed. "Things are different now that school's started."

"Because you have to clean up kids' puke and scrub the toilets?"

"Hmm . . . now that you mention it, there has been one fifth-grade student who's been keeping me pretty busy that way."

"Very funny," I muttered.

"Nah, it's not that," he said. "It's just that before, I felt like I was accomplishing something, making a difference. From now on it'll be nothing but mopping, sweeping, cleaning . . ." He shrugged again. "Routine. Same old stuff, you know? So, today my name is Stuck in a Rut." He cast his line. The sinker hit the water with a *plook*.

I wondered if he was thinking about quitting this job already, too. The old pick-up-the-paycheck-and-quit routine. Life would sure be easier for me if he did, at least at school. But I was hoping Mom could cut back to part-time. She could if Dad would just stay put for once.

"Life gets a little more complicated as you get older," Dad continued. "You'll see. Throwing up at school isn't that bad. Things could always be worse. One day you'll look back on this day and laugh." He cranked the fishing reel. "Don't sweat the small stuff."

Small stuff? He didn't get it. He didn't get any of it. I exploded.

"This is not small stuff!" I yelled, clenching my fists and pulverizing my saltine. My words carried out over the water and bounced off the maple trees on the shoreline. The brightness in his eyes flickered for a second as he looked at me. He was quiet for what seemed like a week. Finally he spoke.

"Am I allowed to change my name? I want to change it to Forgetful Old Fart. I guess I've forgotten what it's like to be a kid."

I snorted. "You sure don't act like you've forgotten."

He lowered his pole, resting it on a rock. "What do you mean by that?"

I had his full attention now. This was my chance to tell him how I really felt. How I was humiliated by the way he acted at school. How he couldn't be my "friend-for-now" until I made a new "friend-for-keeps." I stared at the fishing pole, getting angrier as I thought about all of the embarrassing things he had done. But when I looked up at him and saw the way his eyes were, dark and small and so serious, I knew he was only trying to help. I knew I couldn't hurt his feelings.

"Well," I began as gently as I could, "you haven't forgotten how to jump rope, I noticed."

"Yeah, how about that?" He straightened up, lifted his pole again, and smiled. "Your old man's in pretty good shape, wouldn't you say? I bet not too many of your friends' dads could pull that off."

"I wouldn't know," I grumbled. "You have to *have* friends before you can know anything about their dads."

I quickly fixed my eyes on the fishing pole again. I could feel him staring at me, and a hot, prickly feeling started in my eyes. I blinked fast until the prickles went away. I wanted to say more. I wanted to tell him that I didn't even want a new friend. That I couldn't risk making a new friend because it hurts too much when you lose them. That I just wanted to be left alone. But I couldn't trust myself to get all that out without crying.

It was quiet. A sudden puff of wind made the pine trees swish. The waves slopped. A lone seagull called, "Caw, caw," then swooped and hovered over us. Finally Dad spoke.

"You know how I like to work in the garden? Well, the way I see it, friendship is kind of like gardening. You don't just plant a seed and walk away. You have to tend to the garden, pull a few weeds now and then." He stopped and thought a minute, then added, "A little mulch every so often doesn't hurt either—saves it from drying out completely."

I thought about Tim. I had tended that garden for a long time, and what good had it done me?

"What's the use of spending all that time pulling weeds when the garden dies anyway?" I grumbled.

Dad sighed. "Sometimes, despite all of our hard work, there comes an early frost. Haven't you heard the old saying 'It's better to have loved and lost than never to have loved at all'?"

"It's not true," I said. This time I knew I was right.

I was blinking fast again, trying to get rid of those prickles. I could feel him staring at me. Like a magnet, his gaze pulled my eyes up to meet his and locked them there.

"Friendship is a risky business," he said sadly. "There are no guarantees. But don't let your garden become a jungle."

Darn him! How did he manage to get this conversation so turned around? This was supposed to be about him, not me. He was the one who was acting like an idiot at school, and now I had to sit here and listen to him tell *me* how to act? I should have known better than to try to talk to him when we were stuck out here in this wilderness, this jungle! I couldn't just walk away.

In the car on the way home I dug my pink pad out of my book bag and wrote a note to Tim.

FOR Tim URGENT ☐

FROM Me

MESSAGE How come my dad acts so childish at school when he's supposed to be a grown-up and then acts so much like a grown-up when I need someone who understands like a kid? And where is Tarzan when you need him?

WHEN I AWOKE the next morning, I lay in bed remembering the events of the last couple of days: mystery lunches with Dad, underdoggies at recess, throwing up in class, arguing with Dad at the lake. I decided to stay in bed and lie low until it all blew over. This could take a while.

Why should I get up, anyway? I bet I could think of ten good reasons not to. I made a list in my head.

1. It's a school day.
2. I'll have to eat another peanut-butter-and-jelly sandwich for lunch. (I shivered, thinking about Dad's lunch. Dijon mustard looked like baby poop.)
3. The Cocoa Puffs are all gone.
4. I'm being stalked by a chicken.

5. The bus might not make it over the bridge on Jeffers Road.

6. We're having another spelling test and I can never remember if *tomorrow* has one *m* and two *r*'s or the other way around.

7. I'm in fifth grade and my dad is the school janitor.

8. I'm in fifth grade and my teacher is the school principal.

9. I'm in fifth grade and my best friend isn't.

10. I'm in fifth grade.

I could have gone on, added another twenty at least—ten of which would have included Birdlips—but my alarm broke my concentration. I hit the snooze button and sighed. Maybe I could sleep on the bus on the way to school. But I couldn't trust Diane to wake me up when we got there. Besides, I had to be awake to say my Jeffers Road prayer.

I slid out of bed and went to the window. From here, I could just see the edge of the pine forest peeking up beyond the endless cornfields. Before he got sick, Tim and I used to ride our bikes there every chance we got. It was his favorite spot. We'd pedal as fast as we could, then jump off into the grass, rolling, laughing, letting our bikes crash to the ground. We'd pick cattails from the edges of the ditch, then flip our bikes over and feed the cattails to the spokes of the spinning back wheel, watching the fluff fly and drift off on the breeze.

Now, whenever I walk through that pine forest, it seems as if every pinecone lying there is sticking a hundred little brown tongues out at me.

I padded into the bathroom and looked at myself in the mirror. With my brown hair, brown eyes, and brown freckles, I looked like a pinecone myself. I stuck out my tongue. Today my name is Pinecone Head.

Holding my head under the faucet, I tried to smash down the most stubborn pieces of hair, but I knew I was going to need help. I picked up my favorite barrette, the one with the four roses—one green, one pink, one blue, and one yellow—all lined up in a row. Tim had given it to me for my tenth birthday. I snapped it on, then clenched my teeth and opened my lips, trying to make a smile. The flash of white teeth and the four tiny roses were the only things keeping me from disappearing into the brown bathroom cabinets.

Mom was waiting for me in the kitchen. "Today my name is Gray Guilt," she confessed. "Can I give you a lift?"

At school, I hesitated outside my classroom, bracing myself for an attack by my classmates about my fine display of regurgitated breakfast yesterday. I took a deep breath and went straight to my desk. I slid into my seat, keeping my head down, pretending to be busy putting away my math book. But something was different. I felt exposed, like a wall had been removed. When I looked up, I figured it out. Diane wasn't sitting in front of me anymore. The Wall of Birdlips was gone.

"Over here!" Diane sang out from the desk next to me. I looked over. Tim's seat was no longer empty. It was filled—every inch of it—with Diane.

"What are you doing in Tim's . . . that seat?" I asked. I felt a little dizzy again. What had happened while I was out yesterday afternoon?

Birdlips smiled a thin, evil grin and pointed to Brad. Now that the seat in front of me was empty, I had a good view of the back of Brad's head. Where his long skinny braid had once been, a ragged stubble of hair now bristled. Puzzled, I looked back at Diane. She made a cutting motion with her index and middle fingers.

My mouth fell open as I looked again at the back of Brad's head, then at Diane, horrified. "You chopped off Brad's ponytail?"

She shrugged. "It was right in front of my face. How could I resist?"

"What did Ms. Cordle do?"

Diane rolled her eyes. "She called my parents. They're coming in this afternoon for a conference. Then Brad whined about not trusting me sitting behind him, so Ms. Cordle moved me here."

I shook my head in disbelief at Diane's nerve. So now Birdlips would be sitting next to me instead of in front of me. And I was just beginning to like having the seat next to me empty.

I gasped. The notes! Had Diane found them? Had she read them?

Ms. Cordle waded right into the geography lesson. "The Ohio River flows south from Pennsylvania and eventually joins the Mississippi," she droned. My own river of sweat was flowing south from my armpits as I thought about the notes. What exactly had I written, anyway? And how many had I stuck in there? I studied Diane in quick glances, looking for clues, but she kept her eyes on her book. If she did find the notes—and why wouldn't she?—she had enough evidence to destroy me. All those things Dad did to embarrass me would seem like nothing once Diane blabbed to everyone about me writing notes to dead people. It was like she had my confession in writing. "Yes, I am crazy. A Poetry Therapy failure. A nutcase."

At recess, I headed straight for my oak tree and climbed up, making sure no one saw me. I settled into my usual spot,

straddling the wide branch and leaning back onto the trunk.
I pulled out my pink pad and wrote.

FOR Tim   URGENT ☒

FROM Me

MESSAGE Diane's sitting in your desk. How will I get mes-
sages to you now?

I peeked through the leaves and down at the playground.
Diane was saying something to Audrey, her hand cupped to
Audrey's ear. She must be spreading the news already that
I'm a complete loony tune.

I crumpled the note and crammed it into a knot in the tree,
then climbed down, landing with a *poof* in the soft dirt below.
The huge trunk hid me as I leaned into it, watching for an
opening. This tree was bigger than I realized. Stretching my
arms out as far as they would go, I tried to get my arms around
the trunk. The bark scratched my cheek. I wanted to let go before anyone saw me, but the tree held me there. Finally, break-
ing free from the tree's hold on me, I dashed for the cornfield.
The leaves of the cornstalks sliced at my arms as I breast-
stroked my way through several rows. The earth felt cool

beneath me as I plopped down, hugged my knees, and bit my lip.

Soon the loud clear bongs of the recess bell rang out. *Pull, release, wait,* I said to myself, as if giving instructions to the bell ringer—even if the bell ringer was Dad. *Especially* if the bell ringer was Dad. Pull, release, wait.

Finally, all the ding-dongs on the playground ran inside. I didn't budge. If I didn't go back in, probably no one would notice anyway. I looked at my arms, pale and thin, wrapped around my knees. I was practically invisible anyway. If I didn't go back in, the only difference would be just another empty desk.

The bell stopped ringing, and the laughter and the voices died out. It was quiet. The only sound was the rustling of the breeze through the cornstalks over my head. I looked up. A big, puffy white cloud drifted by.

I remembered one day when Tim and I were lying on our backs in the grass watching the clouds make shapes, then drift away. Tim said to me then, "If you die before I do, peek down from a cloud and wave to me." I said I would and made him promise to do the same if he went first.

Then, one day last summer, I actually did it. I lay down on my back in the grass and looked, for hours, for Tim's small hand to reach out from behind one of those big fluffy clouds. I remembered wishing we had picked a time of day to look and to wave. It would have saved me a lot of looking. But is heaven on daylight saving time or not?

When Mom caught me watching for Tim to wave from heaven, that's when she signed me up for Poetry Therapy. I hadn't put up much of a fight since I didn't have anything better to do anyway, with Tim gone. Somehow I made it through the six weeks of Poetry Therapy, but I was afraid they were going to flunk me because I wasn't cured. I still missed Tim.

I pulled out the pad again. Just seeing the bright pink color made me feel better somehow, like the pink Pepto-Bismol Mom gave me when my stomach was upset.

FOR Tim   URGENT ❑

FROM   Me

MESSAGE I hugged our tree today. I think it hugged me back.

Another note and no way to deliver it. I got to my feet and brushed off my rear, but I couldn't go back to class yet. I needed more time to think.

IN THE PRIVACY of the bathroom stall, I tried to figure out how things had gotten so messed up. First, I lose my best friend, and then my dad tries to take over the school acting like a janitor, a student, *and* a teacher. And now I don't have a way to deliver my notes to Tim. I tried to pace like Dad did. Was this supposed to help you think? There wasn't much room in the stall for pacing. One step, turn. One step, turn.

KERPLUNK.

Oh no. I gazed, horrified, into the toilet. At the bottom of the white porcelain monster, way, way, *way* down there, lay my favorite barrette. I caught a glimpse of the four roses just before the soggy toilet paper floated over and blocked my view. Why did it have to be this barrette? I could have flushed the Pocahontas one without a second thought.

My armpits felt damp. How long had I been gone? Ms. Cordle might come looking for me any minute.

Or would she send Dad?

Wait a minute! That's it! Dad! I was so upset I hadn't been thinking straight. I hurried out of the bathroom and down the hall.

Please let him be in the janitor's office where he belongs for once, I prayed. I didn't have time to look for him if he wasn't there. I pushed open the heavy steel door and scampered down the steps. "Dad?"

"Yes, I am," he announced.

I felt calmer just hearing his voice from out of the darkness.

"I need your help, fast. Come on." I grabbed his hand and pulled him after me. "Hurry up."

As we made our way down the hall to the girls' bathroom, I walked backward and explained to him what had happened. He stopped at the door.

"Wait a minute." He pulled his hand away. "I can't go in there."

"Dad, you're the janitor now, remember? You do your best work in bathrooms. All I have to do is go in first and make sure there's no one in there. Wait here."

He nodded, smiled, folded his arms, and leaned against

the wall. I pushed the bathroom door open and immediately heard the unmistakable sound of a toilet being flushed. Ms. Cordle emerged from the middle stall, adjusting her belt.

"Penelope," she said, "I was looking for you."

I glanced at the stall behind her, desperately trying to remember which one I had used.

"Um . . . I . . . I forgot to wash my hands," I said. Looking down at them, I noticed there *was* cornfield dirt under my fingernails.

"Well, okay, but let's not dawdle. We have work to do." She rinsed her hands and left the restroom. I heard her say hello to my dad as the door swung shut. He wouldn't tell her, would he?

I pushed the door of the middle stall open. Clean. Of course. Ms. Cordle had flushed. I was getting hot again. I moved to the stall on the right.

Clean.

I took a deep breath. Only one more stall left. I felt like a contestant on *Let's Make a Deal*. "So, what will it be, young lady?" I imagined the announcer asking. "Do you want to trade whatever is behind Door Number Three for a brand-new shiny barrette?"

No! I'll take my chances on Door Number Three!

I pushed open the door of the last stall. It banged against

the toilet-paper dispenser. I swallowed, closed my eyes, and crossed my fingers. I stepped up to the edge of the toilet, forced one eye open, and peeked over the edge.

Yes! There it was, still lying at the bottom of the pot. I ran out to tell Dad the coast was clear.

He walked in, entered the stall, rolled up his sleeve, stuck his hand down, grabbed my barrette, and flushed the toilet. I watched his face. He didn't even wrinkle his nose or close his eyes. He strolled to the sink, lathered up his hands and my barrette, rinsed them, then began whistling as he rolled a brown paper towel out of the dispenser.

"Down in the valley, valley so low." He dried off my precious barrette and handed it to me, singing in a low voice, *"Hang your head over, hear the wind blow."*

He ambled to the door, pulled it open, then turned and winked. As the door eased shut behind him, the whistling resumed. *"Hear the wind blow, dear, hear the wind blow,"* then gradually faded as he sauntered back down the hall. *"Hang your head over, hear the wind blow."*

I walked slowly back to my room, turning the barrette over in my hands. It looked as good as new. The four roses looked even brighter after their little bath. Still, I made a mental note not to put it in my mouth again. I entered my classroom quietly and slid into my seat. Ms. Cordle raised an eyebrow.

"Penelope," she began.

Oh, now what? I tried to look innocent. "Yes, Ms. Cordle?"

"Before I forget, make sure you thank your father again for me. My car wouldn't start after school yesterday, and he fixed it. It certainly is nice having such a handy man around."

I managed a small smile. So that was Dad's role. Jack of all trades, master of being around.

❏ 15
BURIED TREASURE

AT NOON I asked Ms. Cordle if I could eat lunch with Dad in the janitor's office. I was pretty sure she would say yes since she was so happy about Dad fixing her car and all. I was feeling a little guilty about yelling at him at the lake, so I thought I'd surprise him and have lunch all set out for him. Besides, lunch in the coal room meant no lunch in the cafeteria. And no chance of any more embarrassing incidents.

Dad was supposed to pass out milk before he took his lunch break, so I would have time to get everything ready. I'd pull his lunch box down from the shelf, spread out a napkin, arrange his food, maybe even pour his coffee for him.

He is going to be so surprised, I thought as I made my way down the four gray steps to the coal room. Down, down, down into my secret hideaway. I turned the corner at the bottom of the steps and jumped.

"Dad!"

He jumped, too, then quickly grabbed a paint-splattered sheet and threw it over a canvas that sat on an easel in the corner.

"What are you doing?" I asked, looking from the covered easel to him, then back again. On a table next to the easel was a jelly jar, half filled with greenish brown liquid and crowded with paintbrushes of various sizes. Tubes of blue, orange, and yellow paint lay squeezed out and twisted on a palette.

"Dad, you're painting! You can't do that at work. Who's handing out the milk?"

"Russell is doing milk duty for me today."

"Oh, well, that's really great," I said as sarcastically as I could. "This way he'll be all trained and ready to take over when Ms. Cordle fires you!"

I turned and ran back up the four gray cement steps to the heavy steel door, feeling again like I was under that tub and suffocating. I pushed with all my might and escaped, but I didn't have anywhere to go. Nowhere to run. There was no way I could eat lunch now, and I wasn't about to go out to recess. I hurried back to my classroom, plopped down at my desk, and laid my head on my arms.

Suddenly I was very confused. Why was I so upset? I thought I didn't want Dad working here as the janitor. He was making a fool of himself and embarrassing me. And now here I was getting upset because I was afraid he was going to be fired. What did I want, anyway?

I wanted him to do his job, that's what I wanted, and for him to do it correctly and quietly without stirring everything and everybody up. Was that too much to ask?

I reached into my desk and pulled out the pink pad.

For Tim	URGENT ☒
From Me	

MESSAGE Mr. "Jack of All Trades" is out of control!
What part of the word JANITOR doesn't he understand?!

But this time writing to Tim didn't make me feel any better. I still had no way to deliver my notes.

After school I trudged up to my bedroom, closed the door, and plopped down on my bed. "Squeaky" squeaked.

"Oh, be quiet," I grumbled. I pulled off my shoes and threw them, hard, in the direction of my closet. They clunked as they hit the cardboard box stored in there. Tim's box.

Slowly I crossed the room, entered my closet, and sank down onto my knees. I stared at the box. Powerful memories were lurking just beneath the flimsy cardboard lid. If I opened it, they were going to leap out and punch me in the stomach. But Tim memories were haunting me anyway. How worse could it get? I took a deep breath and lifted the lid. Everything was still there, just as Tim's mom had packed them: the Matchbox cars, the games, the books. I pulled out the book on astronomy, Tim's favorite. I opened it, stuck my nose deep inside, and breathed. When I pulled it away from my face, I half expected to find myself right there by Tim's big hospital bed again. But no, I was still here, on my knees in my closet, sniffing a book about stars.

Then something else in the box caught my eye. A corner of something gold and shiny stuck out beneath a Frisbee. I reached down and pulled out a small treasure chest. It had a slit in one end, like it was supposed to be a bank, but the top was hinged and opened like a real treasure chest. Inside was a tiny gold key on a chain.

I smiled. Like always, Tim had come up with the answer.

I crawled out of the closet, grabbed my book bag, and pulled out the undelivered notes I had written to Tim. I smoothed them out, folded them in half lengthwise, and placed them in the gold treasure box. Then I locked the box and put the key around my neck. Linda and Audrey had nothing on me now with their "Best Friends" necklaces.

The next morning while all the kids spilled off the bus at school, I ducked behind the big oak tree. With the sharp stone I had used to draw my headless chickens in the dirt, I dug a hole in the soft sand beneath the oak tree and planted the treasure chest. My notes could reach Tim now, buried in a box in the ground just like he was.

I patted the dirt back into place, brushed off my hands, and marched toward the school. The flower bed stopped me. Mulch. What was that Dad had said at the lake? Something about friendships being like gardens and that mulch keeps things from drying out. I scooped up a handful of the loose wood shavings and carried it back to the oak tree. I sprinkled the mulch evenly over the spot where my notes were buried. There. I felt *mulch* better. I ran up the steps to the school, entered my classroom, and slid into my seat. When I yanked out my geography book, a folded piece of paper fell into my lap. I stared at it. It just lay there yawning at me. I looked up at Ms. Cordle. She was taking attendance. I glanced over at Diane's seat. It was empty again. Diane was in the back of the room, sharpening her pencil. I picked up the paper, unfolded it slowly, once, twice, three times, willing it not to crackle, then read the words:

love is more thicker than forget
more thinner than recall
more seldom than a wave is wet
more frequent than to fail

it is most mad and moonly
and less it shall unbe
than all the sea which only
is deeper than the sea

love is less always than to win
less never than alive
less bigger than the least begin
less littler than forgive

it is most sane and sunly
and more it cannot die
than all the sky which only
is higher than the sky

I hope this makes you feel bedder.

My arms felt weak, and I dropped them to my lap, still gripping the note with both hands.

Where did this come from?

I wanted so badly to believe that it had come from Tim, that he had already received my buried notes and was sending a message back. But I knew that wasn't possible.

But who? Birdlips? She was the only one who would have found the notes I had stuffed into the empty desk. But Birdlips? A poem?

I read the poem again. It didn't make much sense at first, but somehow, line by line, it kind of did make sense. In a weird way. In a "mad and moonly" way.

"Love is more thicker than forget, and more it cannot die." That's right. My memories of Tim are so thick, I will never forget him. Those memories cannot die.

Could Birdlips really have been responsible for something so thoughtful? Could she have molted and lost some of her nastiest feathers?

I shook my head. This is so weird, getting a note like this from Diane. She still hadn't even mentioned the other notes I wrote. Could she really be keeping them just between us? Was it possible for Diane to keep her bird lips shut for once?

Dad had also said something at the lake about pulling

weeds to make friends. Maybe Diane wasn't as weedy as I thought. Maybe I should try to include her in something. It would have to be a short something, though, like maybe one game of Four Square. I didn't want to be stuck with her for too long.

I sighed. That's lame. If I'm going to invite her to do something, it should be something good.

Just then the bell started ringing. I checked to make sure Russell was in his seat and not doing that job for Dad, too.

What should I do about this poem? Could I pretend that I just never saw it? See if Diane says anything first?

Ms. Cordle snapped her attendance book shut. I jumped and shoved the poem back into my desk. For now, I'd act as if nothing had happened. I stared out the window. Funny. The sky looked higher than the sky.

WHEN I RETURNED from recess, another note was in my desk.

Your lucky to have your dad around.

There it was again, twice now, that thing about how nice it was to have my dad around. But lucky? She must be kidding. Maybe Birdlips would like to borrow Mr. Jack of All Trades for a day.

Then I thought about Diane's dad. He was never around. Was that why Diane did the stuff she did? Mom said sometimes kids act up just to get attention.

I sighed. Shoot. Maybe I would have to try to be a little

nicer to her. Maybe I should even invite her up into my tree house.

No one but Tim had ever been up there.

I could write her a note and invite her for just a little while.

But sticking a note to Diane in the same place I had put notes to Tim just didn't seem right.

I could just hand her a note, or ask her in person.

But I wasn't ready to make any moves I might regret.

Then, after lunch, I received a note that I couldn't ignore.

You have to be careful when trying to make new friends. You can't get too close to someone too soon because it might be the wrong one. Then your stuck.

P.S. If you want to right back, put the note in the pencil box at the back of the room. Leave a pencil sticking out so I know it's there.

The wrong one? How dare she think I might be the wrong one for her. I have never trapped *her* under a tub or scarfed down all *her* Cocoa Puffs.

I read the note again, getting angrier. This time I didn't even look around to make sure no one was watching me. I gritted my teeth, clenched my pen, and wrote.

FOR _____ URGENT ❏

FROM _____

MESSAGE You know what really makes me mad? People who don't appreciate how good they've got it. Whiners. I hate whiners. I am going to make myself a pin to wear like this: (WHINING⊘) That way anybody who feels like whining will know better than to get in my way.

P. _____

My pen pressed hard on the paper, making the line around the "No Whining" pin so dark and deep the paper ripped. This note couldn't wait. I shoved it into my pocket and went to the pencil sharpener. As I cranked the handle, I looked around. No one was watching. I pulled the note out of my pocket, lifted the lid to Tim's pencil box, and dropped it in. Then I propped the end of a pencil on the edge of the box and replaced the lid. I picked up my freshly sharpened pencil, blew off the pencil shavings, and casually strode back to my seat.

All morning, I watched for Diane to go to the pencil box and get her note. She never budged. When we came back from the C.A.G.M. after art class, the pencil flag was down. My note had been picked up. I couldn't wait to find out what she had to say about that one.

But by the end of the day, no more notes had been delivered to my desk. I checked the pencil box, too. Just pencils.

Maybe I had overreacted a little, pulled the bell over the top. Her note had said something about not wanting to get too close, too soon. I felt the same way. It was hard to believe she and I actually agreed on something.

I wrote a note to Tim.

FOR Tim	URGENT ☒
FROM Me	

MESSAGE If I invited someone over to my tree house, do you think I should warn them about Ares? Or do you think that would just scare them off?

Maybe Diane was just a big coward after all. If my measly little "No Whining" note had scared her off, maybe she was afraid of chickens, too. Maybe she was even afraid of heights. In either case, I'd be off the hook. I decided to take a little survey.

FOR			URGENT ❏
FROM			
MESSAGE			
Are you afraid of heights?	YES	NO	
(Circle one)			
Are you afraid of crazed chickens?		YES	NO

On the way to gym class, I delivered my survey to the pencil box and propped up the pencil-tip flag. After gym, I stayed to help put away the tumbling mats. When I got back to my desk, my survey had already been filled out and returned.

FOR			URGENT ❏
FROM			
MESSAGE			
Are you afraid of heights?	YES	(NO)	
(Circle one)			
Are you afraid of crazed chickens?		YES	(NO)*
*I know how to hypmatize them.			

She can hypnotize chickens? How could I have not known this? Probably because I didn't even know it was possible to hypnotize chickens. My mind was racing. Maybe we could work out a deal: one ticket to my tree house in exchange for the hypnotizing of one crazed chicken. I'd have to be careful how I worded the note, though. How long does it take to hypnotize a chicken? And how long will one dose last?

After finishing the note, I was anxious for an answer. I decided to skip the pencil-box routine and just give the note to her directly. I wanted to find out right away if she could come over and cast her spell on Ares.

"Psst, Diane," I whispered, keeping one eye on Ms. Cordle, whose back was turned. Diane just looked at me, confused.

I held out the note. "Take it!" I rasped.

Finally Diane reached over and grabbed the pink note out of my hand. I watched her read it, lips moving.

FOR Diane   URGENT ❑

FROM Penelope
_____

MESSAGE Do you want to come over to my tree house after
school? It will be open from 4–5 tomorrow only.
_____

Diane looked as if I had just invited her to Disneyland.

"Cool!" she said, waving the note.

Ms. Cordle whirled around, eyes searching the class. I slunk down. Diane shoved the note in her desk and her braid in her mouth.

Suddenly I had this sinking feeling that I had just made a huge mistake. I felt like asking Russell if I could borrow his eraser that said *I never make BIG mistakes* and just rub out the last fifteen minutes of my life. I wanted to say, "Cut!" like they do in the movies and get rid of that last scene of me writing that note to Diane and handing it over.

Diane was looking at the note again. "You didn't have to write me a note about it, though," she whispered. "You could have just asked me." She shrugged. "Whatever. I'll be there. Four o'clock sharp."

When I got home from school, I put the pink pad of *While You Were Out* notes back on the telephone table where they belonged. They were just getting me into more and more trouble.

That night I dreamed I showed up at school in just my underwear—bright pink underwear. It matched my face and the piece of paper Ms. Cordle handed Dad when she fired him in front of my classmates, each of them sporting choppy new haircuts by Diane Scissorhands.

"Wow! I NEVER KNEW you could see so far from up here."

Diane stood, hands on hips, taking in the view from my tree house. I followed her gaze. The view *was* pretty neat.

"Down there at that corner is where Dad and I sell strawberries in the summer," I pointed out. "There's more traffic there."

Diane turned a half circle. "Hey, there's my house! I can even see my swing."

Diane's swing swayed gently from the huge buckeye tree planted in her front yard. That was the best thing about Diane, her swing. The wide, flat wooden seat was worn smooth, so you never had to worry about splinters. The thick ropes holding it up seemed endless. That swing could go higher than any swing I'd ever known. And the ride was smooth and quiet, not like the clanky chain-link swings at school with the uncomfortable rubber U-shaped seats that squished your butt. I could get Diane's swing going so high, my toes touched the leaves of the branches. Then it seemed as if I hung there for a second, suspended in space, before that long swoop back to earth. Whenever I felt like punching Diane, I thought about that cool swing in her yard and counted to ten, sometimes twenty. If I gave her a black eye, she probably wouldn't let me swing on her swing anymore.

Diane made herself comfortable, settling cross-legged onto the floor. Of course Birdlips would feel right at home in a tree. She flipped through Tim's big colorful astronomy book. The tree house seemed like the perfect place to look at it.

I scanned my own yard. Directly below the tree house was the chicken coop. I spotted Ares scratching around in the dirt like a normal rooster. Figures. When someone's around to witness what a rotten egg he really is, he behaves himself. From this high up, I had to admit he looked pretty harmless. From here I couldn't see his comb, ripped and ragged from being frozen winter after winter because he was too stubborn to go into the henhouse. But most importantly, I couldn't see his eyes. Those beady, stone-cold eyes. The windows to his evil soul.

"That's the one," I said to Diane, pointing him out.

"What one?" she asked, getting to her feet.

"The one I want to hypnotize."

Diane snorted. "Hypnotize? You want to hypnotize a chicken?" She giggled, then chortled, then howled, working herself up into a state of hysteria. To add to the dramatics, she leaned over and grabbed her stomach, at the same time releasing her grip on the book. As if in slow motion, it fell. Down, down, down, turning over in the air until it landed with a *plop* and a poof of dust, flat on its back, helpless. The bright blue cover gleamed in the afternoon sun. I groaned.

"Oops," said Diane.

I knew I didn't have time to strangle her immediately. My mind was already racing ahead to the scene I was sure was about to unfold before me. If I moved fast, maybe, just maybe, I could beat him to it. Then I heard it—that chilling, familiar sound. The dull thumping of rooster feet. It was too late.

I'd never seen a chicken run like Ares. He was a regular sprinter. He put the brakes on a few feet from the book, then strutted up slowly, cocking his head and eyeing it.

"Why is that chicken so interested in a book?" Diane asked.

"You don't know Ares," I said. "He's no ordinary chicken."

Just then Ares began pecking away at the bright blue

cover. Slowly at first, then furiously. His beak was making little dents all over it.

"Oh no, oh no, oh no," I moaned.

"You'd better get it quick," Diane said. "He's going to ruin it."

I felt sick. Diane obviously didn't realize the seriousness of the situation.

This chicken was mental.

I took a deep breath, trying to erase all memory of being stalked and hunted by this demented monster. I couldn't let Diane see my fear. I straightened my shoulders and began to climb down. Ares stopped his pecking when he spotted me. He watched me briefly, then began pecking away again.

Hoo boy. This wasn't going to be easy. I bit my lower lip and took one step toward the rooster. He continued drilling the book. This close, the damage was obvious. If I didn't move quickly, Ares was going to make his own black hole.

But a quick move was exactly what I didn't want, especially by him. I stooped very slowly and picked up a handful of gravel, never taking my eyes off of Ares. One by one, I started firing the small pellets at him. He barely noticed. In desperation, I hurled the remaining handful of stones at him, showering him with them. Ares stopped his attack on the book just long enough to make sure the stones weren't something to eat, then he was back at it.

"Oh, now what?" I groaned.

From her safe perch overhead in the tree house, Birdlips squawked, "If that's a library book, the fine is going to kill you."

"If this rooster doesn't first," I muttered.

By now, Ares was pecking the book so hard, he was lifting it right off the ground. I took three brave giant steps toward the bird. Just as quickly, Ares was coming at me, flapping his wings and making a horrible noise. I screamed, covered my head, and ran so fast I thought my legs might leave the rest of me behind. I didn't stop running until I was in my room with the door shut soundly behind me. I plopped down on my bed and hugged my shaky knees.

My book. My beautiful, wonderful-smelling book. Ruined.

Hot, angry tears streamed down my face. She lied to me. She doesn't know anything about chickens, let alone how to hypnotize them. What did she think? That she could just weasel her way into my tree house by lying to me?

I pounded my fist into my pillow. I knew it, I knew it, I knew it, I knew it. I never should have trusted her. When am I ever going to learn? Never again. I'm not trusting anybody ever again.

I flopped onto my back and stared at the Belt of Orion on my ceiling, tears pooling in my ears. My book is destroyed. And by the time I get to school tomorrow, Diane's going to make sure that everyone knows that I'm chicken of a chicken.

I lay there until my breathing slowed and my tears dried. Finally, I sat up and pulled a piece of paper and pencil out of my nightstand.

Ode to a Long Lost Friend (#2)

Nothing will ever be the same any more.
I miss you so much my misser is sore.

❏ 18

IMPRESSIONS

"DAD, CAN I RIDE to school with you today?" I stuck my head into the kitchen, trying to sound casual.

He set his coffee cup down, hesitated. "Well, I guess so, but you'll have to hurry. I'm leaving a little earlier today. I have some work I need to finish up."

"I'll be ready in five," I said, bounding up the stairs. I pulled on jeans and the first T-shirt I could find. I didn't really care what I looked like as long as I didn't have to ride the bus to school with Diane.

When we got to school, I started to follow Dad down the hall to the coal room. He stopped before we got to the door. "Um, since you're here early, why don't you make yourself useful?" he said. "How about straightening the desks for me in each of the classrooms, okay? Line them up all nice and straight?"

I shrugged. "Fine." It was something to do that didn't re-quire any thinking. I started in the first-grade room and worked my way up to my own classroom. By the time I had finished, the buses had arrived.

"Penelope, you're here!" Diane swooped into the class-room. "I was afraid you were sick again."

Suddenly I was beginning to feel that way. What had she told everyone on the bus ride in?

"I've got a present for you," Diane said in a singsongy voice. She approached me with her hands behind her.

I was definitely not in the mood for any more surprises from Diane. I took a step back.

"TA-DA!" she sang, dramatically whipping out the as-tronomy book.

My mouth dropped open. "How did you—"

"That was brilliant," she interrupted, "getting that roos-ter to chase you so I could grab the book. I took it home and cleaned it up. The inside is fine. I think I got most of the gravel out. The cover's just a little bumpy, is all." She ran her hand over it. "It feels kind of cool, really, like the stars on the front are 3-D. And the title feels like it's written in Braille." Diane laughed.

A nice laugh, not a nasty laugh.

"Here," she said, holding the book out to me. "Sorry about dropping it."

I took the book, speechless. Diane wandered over to the fourth graders and began telling them about her exciting visit to my tree house.

Audrey stopped on her way to her desk and raised an eyebrow. "Wow, Penelope, Diane's actually being nice to everyone today. You should invite her over more often. You're like a snake charmer."

Russell rattled by with his marbles. "Yeah, Penelope, if you can calm down Diane, you won't need me to teach you how to hypnotize chickens."

My head spun around to look at Russell. "What did you say?"

Russell's face and ears turned as pink as my *While You Were Out* slips. "Nothing," he mumbled.

I felt like I was just waking up from a fuzzy dream. "Russell? *You* wrote the notes?"

Russell jammed his hands in his pockets. "I just wanted to give you that poem," he explained. "My uncle gave it to me at Tim's funeral. It's kind of a weird poem, made it hard to memorize."

"You memorized that poem? Just so you could give it to me?"

Russell shrugged, turning pink again.

Slowly things started making sense, but I was still confused about one thing.

"Excuse me a minute," I said. I walked over to Diane's desk and stooped to look inside. What a mess. I pawed through the wreckage until I spotted the bright pink papers. There, in the far back, crumpled into the left-hand corner, were the first notes I had written to Tim. Neither Russell nor Diane had ever seen them.

I rescued the notes and smoothed them out on the top of Diane's desk, then opened the astronomy book at random. The heading on page 94 asked DO BLACK HOLES EXIST? I tucked the notes inside.

Hugging my precious book to my chest, I strolled back over to Russell. "Well, *Chief*, I think you owe me one," I said. "Even if Diane *is* being nicer today, I had to put up with her *and* the chicken when neither one of them was being very nice at all."

Russell looked worried. "What do you want me to do?"

"Teach me how to hypnotize a chicken."

"Okay," said Russell. "On one condition."

"What's that?" I asked.

"You have to make me one of those 'No Whining' pins."

I laughed and stuck out my hand. "Deal," I said.

WHEN MS. CORDLE marched into the room, everyone darted for their seats. She took her place at the front of the room, as usual, then waited. After several seconds she looked at her watch, then at the clock on the wall. She cocked her head, as if listening for something. I looked at the clock. Eight forty-five. Uh-oh. Dad should have rung the bell five minutes ago. Suddenly Russell sat up straight, turned in his seat, and looked at me, his face no longer bright pink, but a ghostly white. I wasn't sure what that look meant, but I had a sinking feeling it involved Dad.

Ms. Cordle strutted for the door, heels clicking. I tried to think fast, to think of a way to stall her. I looked again at Russell, trying to say "think of something" with my eyes. Suddenly I heard myself blurt out after her, "I'll go check on him, Ms. Cordle. He probably just got busy doing something else." She dismissed my plea. "Everyone, please get started reading Chapter Two in your history books. I'll be back shortly."

I couldn't just sit there and do nothing. Maybe if she headed for the kitchen to look for him there, I could dash down the hall and beat her to the coal room and warn Dad she was coming so he could hide the evidence that he was painting on the job. I followed her out the door.

But Ms. Cordle didn't head for the kitchen. She headed straight down the hall for the coal room ahead of me, clicking along swiftly, green skirt flowing, a woman on a mission.

She clomped down the steps to the coal room and stopped at the bottom. I peered around the corner to see her put her hands on her hips, then clear her throat loudly to get Dad's attention.

"What is the meaning of this, Mr. Grant?" she asked loudly.

I expected Dad to start falling all over himself, trying to come up with an explanation, an excuse for shirking his duties. I was prepared to be disgusted as he begged Ms. Cordle for mercy. But when I heard his voice, loud and confident, I had to inch closer to make sure the scene in the coal room was the one I had imagined.

I moved down a step so I could see and hear what was happening. Neither of them knew I was there. Just then I heard another voice.

"It's my fault, Ms. Cordle." Russell appeared beside me, breathing heavily. "Mr. Grant asked me to ring the bell this morning. I forgot."

Dad smiled. "It's okay, Chief. I'm all finished. Come on down and take a look. You too, Penelope."

Ms. Cordle turned and frowned at us as Russell and I sheepishly made our way down the rest of the steps into the coal room.

"What do you think?" Dad asked, turning the canvas around to reveal his painting.

I wasn't sure if it was me or Ms. Cordle who gasped the loudest at the sight of the painting. Smiling back at us from the easel was the entire fifth-grade class, including Ms. Cordle. Dad had painted every kid from the waist up, standing in two rows. Our class extended from one end of the canvas to the other. And in the center of the portrait, beaming, was Tim.

Dad broke the silence. "Remember when you tried to teach me Poetry Therapy, Penelope? You told me to keep practicing because, you said, 'you never know when you're really going to need it.' Well, you were right. But I'm an artist. So this is my answer to Poetry Therapy."

He turned to Ms. Cordle. "Mostly I worked on this before and after school and a little bit at lunchtime. Sorry about the bell, but I wanted to finish this today."

I looked at the calendar hanging on the wall. September 12.

"Today is Tim's birthday," I said.

I could tell Ms. Cordle didn't know exactly what to do about all of this, especially with Russell and me standing there.

"We will have to discuss this matter later," she said. "Right now it's way past time we get this school day under way. Russell. Penelope. I will see you two in class. Promptly," she added.

As soon as Ms. Cordle had clicked up the steps and was gone, I stepped up to Dad and threw my arms around his waist, trying with all my might to make my hands meet on the other side of him. I hung on and squeezed like a boa constrictor, my cheek pressing into his soft belly while I stared at the painting.

Dad had painted Tim between Russell and me. Our arms were linked at the elbows.

Suddenly images of last year came flying back at me.

Russell and Tim working on the Civil War project together.

Russell and Tim playing marbles at recess.

Russell and Tim quizzing each other before a spelling test.

And of course the poem that Tim and I had made up on our long bus rides to school had featured Russell in several verses.

I had never thought about anyone else in my class missing Tim. I had been too busy thinking only about me missing Tim.

I released my grip on Dad and turned to look at Russell. He gave me a sad smile. I knew I didn't have to say a word.

"So where will you hang the picture, Mr. Grant?" Russell asked.

"I hadn't really thought about that, Russ. Got any ideas?"

"How about in the C.A.G.M.?" he suggested. "Everybody can see it there."

"Good idea," Dad said, putting his arm around Russell's shoulder. "And maybe we could have a dedication ceremony and rename that room. I never did like calling it the C.A.G.M. anyway."

I began to pace, thinking. Not "cage 'em," but . . . what? Caged was what it felt like under that metal tub. Tight, suffocating. I stopped midpace and looked again at the painting.

"I know!" I said. "Let's call it 'The Elbow Room.'"

"Perfect," said Dad, taking me under his other arm. "Well,

I'd say we've accomplished quite a lot this morning. But there's one more thing we have to do."

"What's that?" I asked.

Dad looked at me, then at Russell. "First one up to the kitchen gets to ring the bell!"

Dad darted for the steps. Russell and I were right on his heels. We passed Dad before he even got to the top. We ran down the empty hall, laughing and glancing back over our shoulders. Dad was right behind us, trying to grab our shirts and pull us back. Rounding the corner into the kitchen, Russell and I arrived at the rope for the bell at the same time, putting on the brakes and sliding the last few feet across Dad's slippery polished floor. I grabbed the prickly rope first. Russell grabbed on next, his hands just above mine. Then Dad arrived and reached up above us both.

"One, two, three, pull!" Dad said.

We pulled. We bent our knees. We released.

I looked at Russell. He was looking up toward the bell, expectantly. Finally, the loud clear tone of the bell sang out. We pulled again.

The bell was swinging smoothly now. The three of us were in sync.

We pulled. We released. We waited. Give and take. Back and forth.

❑ 20
THE LEAST BEGIN

I KNELT NEXT TO my overturned bike at the edge of the pine forest, a stack of cattails at my side. Feeding them into the spinning back wheel of my bike, I churned the pedal.

Sometimes I wish I had never met him at all.

Sometimes I wish we had not seen the frog slide out of the snake's mouth that day last spring when we both thought we would throw up at the sight of it, but we still watched.

Sometimes I wish we had not had to wait for the bus with the blades of grass, wet with dew, stuck to the toes of our shoes.

Sometimes I wish we had not sat side by side on the pea green bench of seat eight on the long ride to school and read the bad words etched on the back of the seat in front of us.

Sometimes I wish we had not slept out under the stars

and heard the burp of the green frogs in the swamp at night, then the first chirps of the birds as the sun rose.

I grabbed another cattail and cranked harder.

WHIRR. WHIRR. WHIRR.

I picked up speed and churned and churned and churned.

The fluff flew up and off on the breeze, more thicker than forget.

THE SCHOOL BUS BAND

by Penelope Grant and Tim Daniels

The rhythm on our school bus is really pretty cool.
We bounce and ping and squeak and sing all the way to school.

Mr. Rockwell drives real fast down the country road.
Bounce. Squeak. Bounce. Squeak. The seats sing from the load.

He makes a stop at Russell's house, then takes off once again.
Russell staggers to his seat. He'll make it, we know he can.

Russell wobbles, grips his lunch box firmly in his hand.
Bang! Bang! It hits the seats. That's our school-bus band.

The rhythm on our school bus is really pretty cool.
We bounce and ping and squeak and sing all the way to school.

Audrey's picked up, then she's tripped up when Dave extends his foot.
Balls and jacks go skittering everywhere you look.

Up and down the hills we go, around the curves we weave.
We lean to the left, then the right, through orange and yellow leaves.

Papers rattle in the breeze past fields of corn and wheat.
Russell's marbles roll around in the tin beneath his seat.

The rhythm on our school bus is really pretty cool.
We bounce and ping and squeak and sing all the way to school.